grass angel

julie schumacher

Delacorte Press

Published by
Delacorte Press
an imprint of
Random House Children's Books
a division of Random House, Inc.
New York

Visit us on the Web! www.randomhouse.com/kids
Educators and librarians, for a variety of teaching tools, visit us at
www.randomhouse.com/teachers

Library of Congress Cataloging-in-Publication Data
Schumacher, Julie.
Grass angel / by Julie Schumacher.
p. cm.
Summary: Rather than go to a spiritual retreat in Oregon with her mother and brother, eleven-year-old Frances insists on staying in Ohio with her odd aunt, but she soon begins to worry that the retreat may really be a cult.
ISBN 0-385-73073-X (trade)—ISBN 0-385-90163-1 (GLB)
[1. Family life—Ohio—Fiction. 2. Aunts—Fiction. 3. Best friends—Fiction. 4. Friendship—Fiction. 5. Summer—Fiction. 6. Ohio—Fiction.] I. Title.
PZ7.S3916Gr 2004
[Fic]—dc21

2003005409

The text of this book is set in 12-point Goudy.

Book design by Trish Parcell

Printed in the United States of America

March 2004

10 9 8 7 6 5 4 3 2 1

BVG

For Emma Lillian
and for Isabella Nan
with love

Acknowledgments

Thanks to Lawrence Jacobs and Alison McGhee, first and best readers; thanks also to my agent, Lisa Bankoff, and to Jodi Kreitzman, who paid at least as much attention to the pages of this book as I did.

chapter one

Summer camp, Frances Cressen understood, was for kids—not for their parents. Parents were supposed to send their kids away for a couple of weeks in July or August and miss them a lot while they were gone. And even though the kids might get lost out in the woods, or almost drown in a marshy lake, or get mosquito bites and poison ivy all over their bodies, they wouldn't miss their parents. Not very much. Their parents were supposed to be missing them.

But Frances' mother seemed to have the whole thing backward. *She* was going to camp. She had signed up for a retreat in Oregon. Two weeks of adult camp at the end of July.

"I don't get it," Frances said. "I thought *I* was going to camp. Here in Ohio."

"You are, but that's earlier. Yours starts on July sixth." Her mother was speaking with a certain determination, a quiet patience. When her mother sounded patient like that, Frances knew that her patience was actually wearing very thin.

"Why are you going?"

"I am going because it's my turn. And because I have the opportunity. You and Everett are coming with me." Frances' mother was a high school English teacher. She always spoke in full sentences. In only eight days, she and Frances would both be out of school for the summer.

"So what kind of camp is it again?"

Her mother sighed. She was doing laundry. She seemed to hate doing laundry. She often accused Frances and her brother, Everett (correctly, of course), of throwing perfectly clean clothes into the hamper to be washed, just so they wouldn't have to put them away. "It isn't a camp, Frances. I already told you. It's a retreat. A spiritual retreat. It's called Mountain Ash."

"So it's just like church." Frances picked up a clump of dryer lint and squeezed it.

"No, it isn't just like church. If it were just like church I could do it at home."

Frances sneezed. Little puffs of lint were floating around in the air in front of her. "I think you *should* do it at home. I want to stay here. I already have my summer planned."

"It isn't too late to change your plans," her mother said. "You need to be flexible."

"I think *you* should be flexible," Frances mumbled, low enough that her mother couldn't hear.

"I thought you might like a change of scenery." Her mother slammed her hip into the dryer, which made it start. "You always tell me that we never go anywhere."

Frances sulked. It was true that she sometimes complained about being stuck in Whitman, Ohio. She had been to Maine once, to see the ocean, and she had been to Washington, D.C., but almost every other day of her life had been spent inside a small red dot on the map, one hundred miles south of Cleveland.

"Two weeks at the end of July?" she asked. Mentally she subtracted fourteen days from her seventy-eight and a half days of summer.

Her mother nodded. "We'll drive there," she said. "We'll see the country. It'll be nice."

Frances subtracted six more days. Fifty-eight and a half days left. "How much Bible study is there?" She had gone to a Bible camp the previous summer. For two hours every afternoon, during the hottest part of the day, she and a dozen other kids had sat in a dusty basement and read aloud from the New Testament. Frances had fallen asleep during the birth of Jesus.

"None. It isn't a Bible camp. It's ecumenical. Nondenominational."

"What?"

"There's no Bible reading," her mother said. She tossed some clothes into the washer, then poured a cup of snowy powder on top.

"Okay, good," Frances said. "But what do we do all day? For two whole weeks?"

"For heaven's sakes, I can't tell you hour by hour, Frances. I'll show you the information. I have some pamphlets. There's a Learning Center, and they have a lake, and there's a children's program that goes up to the age of ten."

"I'll be twelve in September," Frances reminded her.

"They also have a junior baby-sitting program for people your age."

Frances didn't like the way her mother said "people your age," as if Frances was only an acquaintance, one of a large number of eleven-year-olds whom her mother had met. "I don't want to baby-sit all summer. I already baby-sit for Everett." Using her toe, she carved an *F* for Frances into a little pile of soap flakes that had landed on the floor.

"You very rarely baby-sit Everett," her mother said. "Besides, that doesn't count. He's your brother."

"If it doesn't count, I guess I don't need to do it, then," Frances said.

Her mother rested both hands on the edge of the dryer and looked down at its metal surface. Frances knew she was counting—at least to ten, and probably twenty—so that she wouldn't shout or say something she might later regret. Frances thought about taking back what she had said. Sometimes she felt as if a small and terrible person lived inside her and spoke with an ugly voice and had only ugly things to say.

"I think we should talk about this later," her mother said.

Frances said she didn't care if they ever talked about it at all.

They didn't for several days. But the subject came up again on Sunday, when Frances' mother wasn't home. She had been gone for only fifteen minutes when Frances' aunt Blue slammed through the door. "Tell me about Oregon," she said.

Frances looked up from the kitchen table, where she was reading the comics. Her mother had left her a note asking her to empty the dishwasher and sweep the floor, but she had tucked it under the sugar bowl and ignored it. "What about Oregon?" she asked. She wasn't particularly happy to see her mother's sister. Aunt Blue was clumsy and weird, and she sometimes said rude things about Frances' mother. She came over only on Sundays, when Frances' mother was at church. Everett and Frances used to go to church, too, but they had changed congregations so many times in the past few years that their mother had decided to let them stay home to avoid being confused.

"I heard you were going there this summer," Blue said. "I just wanted to hear it from the horse's mouth." She set a white paper bag in the middle of the page that Frances was reading.

Whenever Blue visited, she brought donuts, which Frances knew her mother wouldn't approve of. Her mother hadn't bought or eaten anything with sugar in it for several years.

At the sound of the bag opening, Everett raced into the kitchen in his truck-and-train pajamas, his straw-colored hair sticking up in tiny haystacks. He tore at the white paper sack and stuffed part of an enormous chocolate éclair into his mouth.

"There's got to be something to tell me," Blue said. "Are both of you looking forward to the trip?" She began unrolling a cinnamon roll with her fingers. Blue lived alone in a sagging house behind Whitman's graveyard, and made a living doing something with computers. She worked at home. She was "brilliant. Amazingly bright," Frances' mother always said. "But awkward with people. She's very shy."

"It doesn't matter if we're looking forward to it or not," Frances said.

"Donut, Frances?" Blue was talking with her mouth full. Unlike their mother, who was neat and organized and exact, Blue was big and careless. Frances thought she dressed like a gas station attendant. As usual, her long gray and black hair was loose, and badly combed.

"No."

"I'll have another one," Everett said. He still had half an éclair in his hand, but he reached for a second. "Mom's with the Quakers today."

"Quakers." Blue looked at Frances. "Is that something new?" Frances could tell she was trying not to say anything critical. The week before, Frances had shouted at her because Blue had called Frances' mother *fickle*. Later, Frances had looked the word up: *Changeable*, the dictionary said. *Not reliable or steady*.

"She only goes there once in a while," Everett said. "She's trying them out. They have Meetings. Have you ever been there?"

"No. I'm not a churchgoer," Blue said. "Your mother makes up for my not going at all. How many churches do you think she's been to this year?"

"Why does that matter?" Frances asked. "Why can't she belong to as many churches as she wants?"

"She can," Blue said. "If it makes her happy."

Frances scowled. Of course her mother was happy. She had a job and a house, and she had two kids. What else did she need? The interest in different religions was a kind of hobby, that was all. Personally, Frances would not have used the word *fickle*.

"I think it's six this year," Everett piped up. "Six different churches. I'm counting the school year."

"I don't think it was six," Frances said. She wanted to hit Everett. Probably she would hit him when Blue was gone.

"Six." Her aunt seemed to think the number over. "And how many in the past few years?"

"I know." Everett raised his hand. He was only seven, but he was in third grade already; he had skipped first.

Blue set three glasses on the table and carefully filled each one with milk, dribbling a bit on Frances' sleeve. In addition to being larger than Frances thought women were supposed to be, Blue was a klutz in the kitchen, and twice she had chipped plates while she was visiting. Now she moved around the room as if the floor were made of glass. "Go ahead, Everett."

"Catholic," Everett said. "Presbyterian. Episcopal." He

had cream filling on his fingers, which he held up as he ticked off the names.

Frances didn't remember the Catholic church, and she hadn't liked the Presbyterian Sunday school because the boy who had sat behind her in class had always kicked her chair. Her mother had told her once that in church a person should be able to close her eyes and feel as if she were a link in the chain that made up the world. Frances had simply felt that Charlie Segmeyer was going to kick her chair very slowly around the globe.

"Lutheran," Everett said. Everett had a wonderful memory. Frances suspected that, even though he was almost four years younger, he was much smarter than she was. This seemed unfair.

"Unitarian. Jewish," Everett said. "Last year she belonged to a synagogue."

Blue bit into a donut; sugar dusted her upper lip like a mustache.

"Methodist," Frances said, despite herself. "Baptist." Frances had liked the Methodist church for its music and its stained glass, and the Baptist church for its perfect white paint and for the sermons of the Reverend Dyson, whose bald head had gleamed like a fleshy bulb in the center aisle.

"Jehovah's Witnesses," Everett said. "Quakers. Buddhists."

"How long did the Buddhists last?"

Frances tried to remember. In a drawer in the hall table

were at least a dozen membership applications to Whitman's many houses of worship. Frances didn't think the White Leaf Zen Buddhist Center application had been filled in.

"Oh, and Congregational," Everett said. "It's lucky there are a lot of different churches here. Otherwise she'd have to commute."

Frances told him to be quiet and handed him a napkin for his hands. Actually, she had suggested the Congregational church herself, because her best friend, Agnes, was a member there.

"Why do you think she does it?" Blue asked. She looked at the clock. It was eleven-thirty. In half an hour she would pack up the leftover donuts in the white paper bag and take them home. "Have you thought about it?"

Frances found that, despite her determination not to touch what Blue had brought them, she held a large apple fritter, at least half eaten, in her hand. "No," she said.

Everett smiled at their aunt and shrugged. Unlike Frances, he never lost his temper or got upset, and he got along well with both their mother and their aunt. He was a strange kid, overall. He didn't have many friends and didn't seem to need them. He spent most of his free time playing with a series of three-inch multicolored rubber creatures, so specialized and so rare that no one else in town owned a single one. He kept a large metal tin of the creatures in his closet, and for each of them he had memorized a different set of habits, magic abilities, and plans.

Frances often heard him lifting the metal lid, whispering instructions to them late at night in his room.

Blue poured herself another glass of milk. "You don't mind staying home alone on Sundays?"

"No," Everett said. "We get to eat donuts."

"What about you?" Blue turned to Frances. Though Blue didn't talk very much, she had what Frances' mother called a searching gaze. Her green eyes were like matching streetlights.

"I'm eleven. I'm old enough to stay here without her."

"I guess that's right," Blue said. "You are."

"These are even better than last week's donuts," Everett said, his mouth full of cream. "Will you come out and visit us in Oregon?"

"I don't know," Blue said. "I guess that depends on how long you decide to stay there."

Something in Frances' stomach turned over. "What do you mean *how long*?"

"We're staying two weeks," Everett said. "Our mom decided."

Blue didn't even look at him. Her searchlight eyes were directed at Frances. "What if it was a month?" she asked. "Or a little longer?"

Everett wandered off, bloated like a tick, Frances thought, to watch TV.

Blue continued to look at Frances in a piercing way. This was just like her, to say something unpredictable, something that didn't make any sense. It was one of the things about her that drove Frances crazy: She would drop a bomb into the middle of a regular conversation and then clam up and refuse to say anything more.

Frances could feel anger stretching out like a coil inside her. Summer was the time of year she looked forward to the most. Her mother didn't work during the summer. She wasn't crabby from grading stacks of papers, and she didn't nag Frances about doing homework. The days were graceful and long, the heat seeming to loosen them from the calendar. Frances was counting on endless stretches of laziness, uninterrupted by schedules and plans. She hadn't really agreed to go to Oregon at all. "*If* we go, we'll go for two weeks," she said, trying to keep her voice calm. "You don't know anything about it."

Her aunt dusted some sugar off her cheek with the back of her hand. "Maybe next week you and Everett can come to my house. You can have your donuts over there."

"I don't think so," Frances said. She didn't want to go to Blue's. She hadn't been there very often, partly because Blue didn't invite them, and partly because Frances' mother thought the house was filthy. The main floor was full of computers and computer parts, and stacks of old newspapers and other junk. And the house was small. There was only one tiny bedroom, on the second floor—an attic, really. Frances' mother said that only Blue could sleep in a room that heated up like an oven in the summer and froze during the other parts of the year.

"Here is fine, too," Blue said. "Breakfast probably tastes the same wherever you eat it." She stuffed the donut remnants into the bag, wiped off the table, and stood up.

Everett was singing in front of the TV.

"I don't have to go anywhere this summer, if I don't want to," Frances said, but no one was listening. Everett was singing his nonsense song, and Blue was making her way across the lawn with her bag of donuts, the screen door slamming shut behind her.

chapter two

Frances' best friend—her only real friend—was Agnes McGuire. Agnes was pale and freckled and so thin that Frances sometimes imagined she could see her bones through her flesh. They would be long and bluish white, the color of skim milk. Agnes lived with her parents and an ancient sheepdog named Oops about three blocks from Frances' house. She and Frances had been friends since the second grade.

"Just tell your mom you aren't going," Agnes said. "She didn't give you enough notice. And you don't know anyone in Oregon." They were sitting on Agnes' front porch, in the shade of the lilacs. It was a Tuesday afternoon, warm and sunny and lazy; there were only two more days until the end of school.

"She thinks I'm going to baby-sit all day while she goes hiking or swimming or something," Frances said. "And there isn't going to be anyone out there who's near my age."

"Hey, wait a minute," Agnes said. "You're still going to

be here for Camp Whitman, aren't you? Don't tell me *that's* when she wants you to go to Oregon."

"No, I'll be here. Camp Whitman's earlier," Frances said. She pulled a fistful of lilac buds from the tree and crushed them between her fingers. A thick fragrance filled the air all around them. It smelled like the perfume of a hundred old ladies.

"I hope so," Agnes said. "Because you told me you were going to be here. I gave up that horse camp in Kentucky."

"I know."

"A *sleep away* horse camp," Agnes went on. "Where every single kid was guaranteed their own horse. My parents told me I could pick one camp. And I told them I wanted to go to Camp Whitman with you."

Frances wiped her hands on her shorts, but the lilac smell clung to them. "We can ride horses at Camp Whitman," she said. "Remember last year at camp when we went on that hike, and you and I took the wrong path and got lost until after lunch? You told the counselors that we caught a rabbit and ate it."

"They almost believed me," Agnes said.

"And we can go rock climbing and rafting," Frances added. "Last year we weren't old enough."

Out in the yard, Oops lifted his woolly head to bark at a squirrel, then went back to sleep in the shade of a walnut tree.

"What kind of religious camp is it, anyway?" Agnes asked. "I mean, the one your mom wants to go to. It's not Episcopalian, is it?"

"No." Frances pinched her. Agnes thought Episcopalians were dangerous, because her next-door neighbor, Mrs. Hiffman, was one. Mrs. Hiffman had only one eye, and she screamed like a parrot whenever anyone rang her doorbell. "It's some kind of retreat. It's religious, I guess, but not a religion."

"I don't get it," Agnes said.

Frances said that she didn't get it either. She found a ladybug on the step and carefully picked it up with her thumb. "Your parents don't do stuff like this," she said. "They don't change their minds about things."

"Parents don't have minds," Agnes said. "They're a race of robots sent to earth to control all the people under seventeen."

"I'm being serious," Frances said. "I think when you're a parent, you should try to make things easier for your kids. You should try to make things fun." The outer shell on the ladybug's body opened to reveal a pair of delicate black wings.

"At least you have Everett," Agnes said. "I'm the only child of two people who take classes in how to be parents. They actually have books around the house about how to raise me: *Your Three-Year-Old. Your Five-Year-Old.* Luckily, I think they're only up to age seven."

Agnes' mother came out to the porch to get the mail. "Hello, Frances," she said. "How are things at your house?"

"Don't ask her," Agnes said. "It's not a good time."

"Well. All right. I'll ask her later." Mrs. McGuire sorted

through the mail. "Why don't the two of you find something to do?" she said. "You could go for a bike ride."

"No," Agnes said. "It's too hot."

"Why don't you walk into town?"

"Because there's nothing to do there," Agnes said. "We live in Whitman."

"There's nothing wrong with living in Whitman. It's much nicer than plenty of other places."

Agnes sighed and kicked Frances gently. Mrs. McGuire was short and plump, and when anyone insulted the town she was born in, she seemed to puff up, like a fish. She began a little speech about Whitman, Ohio, that Frances and Agnes had both heard before: It might be a small town, but it was safe, and it was clean, and it was a place where a person could find at least one of everything. There was one grocery store, one hardware store, one movie theater, one ice cream shop, one beauty parlor, one bowling alley, one photography studio, one bakery, one diner, and one beautiful green golf course, which had won several prizes. "I like to think of it as a Whitman sampler," she finished, "just like the chocolates."

"You're allergic to chocolate," Agnes said.

Her mother clamped the lid of the mailbox shut. "I may be allergic," she said, "but I know how to appreciate fine chocolate just the same."

Later that afternoon, before dinner, Frances decided to ask her mother about summer clothes. There were a lot of things she needed. Two new bathing suits, for starters, a pair of sandals, at least one pair of sunglasses, a decent-looking beach towel instead of the stupid ones in the closet, and some new sneakers. "And we should look at the list of things I'll have to buy for camp."

Her mother put two bags of groceries on the kitchen table. "Everett!" she called. "I need you to bring some things in from the car. Frances, you can help me put this food away."

"I remember last year they said I needed hiking boots," Frances said. "I never got any and I could have tripped and killed myself."

Her mother was unpacking the first bag: skinless chicken breasts, fish, milk, eggs, vegetables, orange juice, and low-fat ice cream. She always brought the cold bags in first; there would be three other bags. Frances could guess what each of them contained.

"Everett!" her mother yelled.

Frances poked a finger into the flesh-colored chicken. "And I might need water shoes, too. Last year the twelve-year-olds went white-water rafting."

"Last year you complained about camp," her mother said. "You told me the arts and crafts were silly."

Frances didn't remember complaining about camp, but maybe she had. Still, she had loved Camp Whitman. Complaining about the spidery bathrooms and the mosquitoes was simply a part of the experience. "Agnes says they might have a water trampoline this year," she said. "And they're going to have at least a dozen horses."

Her mother opened the refrigerator, the light inside the machine casting a glare across her face. "I've been meaning to talk to you about something."

The hairs on Frances' arms stood up.

"I know we've talked about going to Oregon for only two weeks," her mother said.

"But we haven't really decided yet," Frances said.

Her mother closed the refrigerator. "I'd like to go for a bit longer. I know you have plans. I know this is happening at the last minute. But it's important to me." She turned around. "I tried to register for the two-week session, but now it's full. The only open sessions last for six to eight weeks—most of the summer."

"So that means we can't go." Frances could feel herself beginning to tremble, as if a rubber band inside her was vibrating, hard. "Because *I'm* going to camp. It's already paid for."

"No, it's not. I only gave them a deposit." Her mother set six green bananas in a bowl on the counter. She always bought six: two for Frances, two for Everett, two for herself. "You've never been out to the West Coast."

"That's because I don't want to go! And I especially don't want to go to Oregon. I can't even name a city there." The rubber band inside her was throbbing, ready to snap.

"Portland," her mother said. "Salem. And keep your voice down. Do you remember I showed you the brochure? Did you read it?"

Frances hadn't looked at it. "Yes," she said. "I thought it was stupid."

Her mother opened and closed the freezer.

"Everett isn't going to want to go, either," Frances said, remembering that she had meant to talk to Everett about this very point: that he should say no when their mother asked him if he wanted to go to Oregon. She could see Everett through the kitchen window. He had stopped halfway to the car to examine something on the sidewalk. Probably a broken robin's egg, an ant, a worm. Everett always stopped in his tracks for nature.

"I'm sure Everett's willing to be flexible," her mother said. "He's open-minded."

Of course, Frances thought. Everett was always open-minded. He was the cheerful and agreeable child, the one who had never cried when he was a baby, whereas Frances had apparently cried for hours every day during her first six months. Everett, their mother always said, was even-tempered like his father. *Who am I like?* Frances had asked her once. Without hesitating, her mother had answered, *You're like Aunt Blue*.

Now Frances sagged into a kitchen chair, kicking her legs. "I'm not going," she said. "I'm staying here."

Everett finally appeared with his first bag of groceries. As usual he had opened the box of saltless saltines and filled his mouth with them. Once his mouth was fully dried out, he would try to whistle.

Their mother waited for him to leave; then she took

hold of Frances' wrists. "I'm not sure I can explain this to you," she said, speaking softly and slowly as if she were trying her words out for the first time. "I work hard all year. I'm a single parent and a good teacher. And at the end of the year I feel hungry. I feel like I'm hungry for some kind of food, but I don't know what it's called or what it looks like."

Frances looked around at the groceries. Generally her mother ate very little. Food didn't seem to bring her joy.

"To some people I suppose it isn't going to make much sense," her mother said. "But I need to do this. Mountain Ash has a wonderful program. Everyone works. Everyone takes part and has a job. There's a dining hall, and there are acres of woods—"

"I don't want a job," Frances said. She pulled away.

Everett walked into the kitchen with another bag. His gold-rimmed glasses shone in the sunlight, so that he appeared to have two disks on his face in place of eyes. "Those birds with the crests on their heads. Are those cormorants?"

"Not in our yard." Their mother helped him lift the groceries onto the table.

"I need to look them up in my bird book." Everett paused on his way out the door. "What are you talking about? You're so serious."

"I'll tell you later." Their mother kissed him on the forehead, even though, judging from the scrapes and the dirt on the paper bags, he had dropped the groceries more than once.

Frances rubbed her arms; there were finger marks where her mother had held on to her, too tight. "It's my summer," she said. "I'm too old for you to just drag me across the country."

"I'm not going to drag you," her mother said.

"Well, good. Because I should get to do what I want."

"Life isn't about getting to do what you want." Her mother folded up the paper bags.

"What is it about, then?" Frances asked.

"These go in the bathroom." Her mother handed her the soap and the toilet paper. "When I find out the answer to that question, I'll let you know."

That night, Frances' bedroom door was open, and she could see from the head of her own bed to Everett's across the hall. Usually she faced the opposite direction, because Everett talked to himself as he went to sleep, or marched his little rubber creatures through the air.

"Everett," she whispered. "Are you asleep?"

"No," said Everett. "I was practicing lying still with my eyes open."

Frances didn't bother to ask him why. Everett had habits that no one understood. "Is Mom in her room?"

Tucked in a shadow, Everett nodded.

"Has she told you anything about this summer? About going to Oregon?"

"Only a little bit," Everett said. "Oregon is the thirty-third state."

"I'm going to tell her that you and I aren't going," Frances said. "I'll run away if she tries to make me go. All they do out there is some kind of Bible study, without the Bibles."

There was a pause, and Frances wondered whether Everett had fallen asleep. Finally he said, "I heard Mom crying on the phone."

"When? Today? Why was she crying?"

"Yesterday," Everett said. "She must have been sad."

Frances leaned back against the pillow.

"Tell me a story," Everett said. Sometimes when he had trouble falling asleep, he liked to have Frances tell him something about their father. He had died when Everett was two and Frances was six. He had been older than their mother, but not *so* old: almost fifty-four. He had died in the basement at his workbench, a nail clutched tightly in his hand.

He had been building a birdhouse. Frances didn't remember seeing it, but she used to ask her mother to describe it for her. The birdhouse was big, her mother said. It had a copper roof, a dozen perches, four separate holes for exit and entry, a wooden trough for food, and even a bird-shaped weather vane. No one knew what had happened to it. Sometimes Frances looked at other peoples' birdhouses and liked to imagine that she could fly through their tiny doors and find her father waiting for her there.

"What do you want me to tell you?" she asked. She heard her mother's bedroom door open; the light went on in the bathroom down the hall.

"Tell me about The Tin Drums." Everett turned over. He didn't remember their father's music store, but he always liked hearing about it.

"The Tin Drums was a great place," Frances said. "He used to bring us there sometimes and we'd play the pianos. He bought me a clarinet when I was five." Frances still wasn't very good on the clarinet. Her teacher, Mr. Mundy, said that her fingers were stiff. "Dad had a saying that he framed and hung on the wall—something about happiness and sadness not making noise, and that's why music had to be invented." Only a month after their father died, The Tin Drums had been turned into a coffee shop.

"Dad was fun," Everett said. "Wasn't he?"

"He was," Frances said. "He liked to do things. He loved making snowmen. He used to write messages in our pancakes."

Their mother finished up in the bathroom, turned out the light, and went back to her room.

"I wish I remembered that," Everett said. "I just remember you telling me about it. It's not the same."

True, Frances thought. Everett had been too young. He had cried for days after the funeral, but now (he had told Frances) he couldn't even remember what their father looked like unless he was standing in front of the photograph in the hall. Frances remembered, sort of. But sometimes she had to look at the photograph, too, to be sure.

"Everett?" Frances asked. "Who was Mom talking to when she was crying?"

No answer—just the whistling noise Everett's nose made when he slept.

Frances turned over several times, then gave up trying to fall asleep and got out of bed. The door to her mother's room was closed, but a rectangle of light was seeping out from underneath it. Frances stood still and listened. On the other side of the closed door she could hear her mother talking quietly, urgently, on the phone.

chapter three

The next night after dinner Frances' mother made Everett and Frances sit down with a pile of books at the kitchen table, even though there was only one more day of school and neither of them had homework. Then she sat down between them to grade her students' papers. Frances knew that the older kids in town thought of her mother as a strict grader and a disciplinarian. The hardworking students at Whitman High School loved her; the less talented hoped to be assigned a different teacher for English 9. Though Frances knew she would never be in her mother's class (the district didn't allow it), she suspected that she was the kind of student her mother would dislike: relatively smart but not ambitious. Her mother hated the idea of talent going down the drain.

"Just *look* at this," her mother fumed, a cup of coffee and a stack of papers at her left hand. "This young girl could easily be an A student, but look at her work!"

Frances looked up from *Misty of Chincoteague*, a book she had read at least a dozen times. She examined the essay in front of her mother. *Robt. E. Lee was a*

Confederate General in the War. He had a lot of different reasons for fighting. In the biography I read for this assignment . . .

"She abbreviates Lee's first name!" Frances' mother shook her head. "And she doesn't even name the war he fought in! Or give the title of the biography! Unbelievable."

Frances said nothing. She knew the student—an older sister of a girl in her own class—and didn't see why abbreviations were a bad idea. They were shorter. They saved time. That's why people used them. But her mother wanted everything to be done the long way. The hard way. And with perfect grammar.

"Ridiculous," her mother said. She gave the student a C-.

"That's a pretty bad grade," Everett said, looking up from the chart he was making about praying mantises and crickets. "Is that what she's getting for the whole year?"

"She'll be lucky to get a C for the year." Their mother got out her grade book. "She should have worked harder."

In her mother's mind, Frances thought, the perfect student was probably not only hardworking and talented and bright but also flexible and even-tempered. Not moody like Frances, whose teachers often called her an underachiever. According to her mother's specifications, the only person who would never disappoint would be someone like Everett.

Frances went back to chapter two of *Misty*. Her mother hadn't said anything about Oregon since the day before.

Maybe she was disappointed about Frances refusing to go to Mountain Ash. She'd probably had to call and cancel their reservation. It served her right. Next time, Frances thought, her mother wouldn't make plans without checking with her first.

She watched her mother award two more C's and a B+ and, finally, lips pressed together, a single A. It was after eight-thirty. Everett had finished his chart and gone to bed. Frances announced that she was going to watch TV.

"No. Clarinet practice," her mother said. "You haven't practiced since the weekend."

"But I'll keep Everett awake."

"Not if you close the door to your room." Her mother made a series of neat check marks in her grading book. "Thirty minutes," she said. "I'll time you."

Frances took her clarinet and music to her room. She propped the music on her dresser and played some scales to warm up, then worked on a couple of older pieces before trying out "Spring Sonata," which still sounded terrible whenever she played it.

"Don't think about your fingering," Mr. Mundy told her. "Pay attention to the music." Mr. Mundy always said that if Frances practiced long enough, she would learn to forget about her fingers and her lips and about the difference between herself and the instrument. The sound of the clarinet would seem to come toward her from every direction. It was what he called "being inside the music." But Frances seemed to be permanently locked outside it, without a key.

She played for a few more minutes, then realized that she had left her assignment book in the hall. She opened the door and heard voices. "No, of course she isn't happy about it," her mother said. "She's at a difficult age."

"Everyone's at a difficult age," a voice answered. "You still seem to be fairly difficult yourself." It was Blue. What was she doing in the kitchen on a Wednesday night?

"I didn't ask you to come here." Frances could hear the squeak of her mother's mop. Mopping floors was something her mother did when she was annoyed. "We could have settled this on the phone. I'm making the best choices I can make, under the circumstances."

"What *are* the circumstances, Anna-Louise?" Frances' mother was always Anna-Louise, never Anna.

There was a silence. They had probably heard her stop practicing. "I'm going to take a bath, Mom," Frances yelled. She quickly crossed the hall and turned on the water in the tub. She slammed the bathroom door, then tiptoed back to her place at the top of the steps.

"You're grabbing at straws," Blue said. "Every month it's something different. Judaism. Buddhism. Meditation. Now Mountain Ash, whatever that is. What's going to be next?"

The mop was squeaking a little faster. Her mother said something that Frances couldn't hear.

"Those are *your* choices," Blue said. "But what about hers?"

The phone rang and her mother answered it. Frances crouched in the hall, a cramp in her leg, waiting.

"You might want to turn off that water now," Blue said. She was standing in the spill of light from the kitchen, looking up at Frances. "I'll bet it's ready to overflow."

Frances stood up, rubbing her leg. She turned off the bathwater, which was icy cold; she had only turned on one faucet. When she got back to the hallway no one was there. "Mom?" She walked down the six carpeted steps and into the kitchen and found her mother and her aunt at the table, the linoleum around them glistening and clean.

No one said anything at first. Blue and her mother were looking down at the wooden surface of the table as if something they needed to say to Frances was written there.

Finally her mother said, "I was telling your aunt Blue about Mountain Ash."

Frances' face went hot. "What about it?"

Blue was picking dirt from beneath her nails.

"I've thought a lot about this, Frances," her mother said. "I've thought about putting it off until next summer. But I don't think waiting makes any sense. Not for me. I need to do this . . . now."

"You can't," Frances said. "You have to give Everett and I more notice."

"Everett and me," her mother corrected her.

The floor was still wet. Her mother and her aunt sat at the table as if on an island that Frances couldn't reach.

"I'm sorry you feel so strongly about this," her mother

said. "But I feel strongly, too. I've written a check for the retreat. For the whole summer in Oregon."

Frances felt as if she'd been running; she had to catch her breath. "I'm going to camp with Agnes this summer," she said. "I'm not going to Oregon. And Everett isn't going, either."

"Everett isn't signed up for camp," her mother said.

Frances felt a small jolt of surprise. This was true; Everett supposedly didn't *need* to go to camp. Unlike Frances, he was able to entertain himself very quietly at home, creating weird but tidy projects out in the yard or around the house.

Blue stood up. "I don't think I should be a part of this conversation right now. Call me, Anna-Louise."

"You can't hire a baby-sitter for the whole summer," Frances said, ignoring Blue. And then she looked at her mother's face and the truth broke over her head like an egg: Everett was going. Everett could stare at a bunch of bugs in Ohio or Oregon or Timbuktu.

Blue stepped out into the night, closing the door quietly behind her. Her boots had left a series of murky footprints on the floor.

"I wish it could be different, Frances," her mother said. "But I don't want you to go if you're going to be so angry about it. I've thought it over, and this is the best arrangement that I can come up with."

"What arrangement?" Frances realized that her voice was much too loud. At times like this her mother often said something about her *tone*, as if Frances were a kind of instrument.

Her mother squeezed out the mop and erased Blue's footprints. "The programs are mainly for younger children. You were right. They're geared toward people Everett's age, at least in the summer. I think it's probably different during the year. In any case, I understand that for you it's harder. You're older. You've made commitments. You have camp."

Frances' mouth was hanging open. She had to make an effort to close it before she spoke. "You and Everett are going? For the whole summer?"

Her mother nodded.

"Just you and Everett. And you're going to leave me here. By myself."

"No, of course not," her mother said. "You're going to stay with Aunt Blue."

chapter four

“You’ve got to be kidding,” Agnes said. They were lying on their stomachs on Frances’ bed, their four bare feet just touching the window. “She’s making you stay with your aunt? She doesn’t even like your aunt. Neither do you. Why don’t you ask if you can spend the summer at my house?”

“I already did.” Frances’ big toe found a hole in the screen. “She said it would be too much trouble for your parents. She said she doesn’t know them well enough to ask.”

“I know them pretty well,” Agnes said. “I’ve been living with them for eleven years.”

“That doesn’t matter.” Frances widened the hole with her toe. “She won’t change her mind. And I don’t care, anyway. She can do whatever she wants. She can drive off to Oregon or go surfing in Hawaii for all I care.”

“Your mother knows how to surf?”

“No.” Frances rolled over. “Never mind.”

Agnes ran her fingers through the dark blue rug. She found several pennies and a jelly bean and handed them to Frances. "So you won't mind living with your aunt? I mean, for the summer?"

Frances shrugged. She was trying not to think about sleeping next to Blue in the tiny attic, rolling over to the rhythm of her snores in the stifling heat.

Frances' mother walked past the open bedroom door with a pair of suitcases. Agnes smiled and said, "Hi, Mrs. Cressen," and then turned an astonished face toward Frances. "Are they packing already? I thought they weren't leaving until next week."

"They're leaving in three days," Frances said. "They're stopping at a rock museum along the way."

"A rock museum?" Agnes picked at a scab on her wrist.

"Everett wants to see it," Frances said. "He read about it somewhere in a stupid book."

Her mother walked past the open door again. "Did you put your laundry away, Frances?"

Frances didn't answer. She began pulling pieces of synthetic fuzz from her bedspread, which her mother had specifically asked her not to do. Her laundry was piled on top of her dresser. A mix of dirty clothes and shoes and books covered most of the floor.

"Do you want me to help you clean up?" Agnes asked.

"No." Frances plucked some more fuzz from the bedspread. "You know, I've heard that kids who go to boarding school have people who do their laundry for them and make their beds and stuff like that. And they don't see their families for months."

"You don't seem like the boarding school type," Agnes said.

Frances was about to disagree, but she looked up and saw Everett standing in the doorway. He was so quiet. Not like Frances, whose footsteps, their mother said, could be heard half a mile away.

"Have you seen my refracting telescope?" Everett was short for his age, but had an older person's way of speaking. Frances thought he looked like a scientist trapped in a tiny body.

"No," she said. "Anyway, you can't use a telescope now. It won't work in broad daylight."

"Why not?"

"You won't see the stars."

"On the opposite side of the world they're using telescopes."

"Everett, you don't live on the opposite side of the world." Sometimes, though, Frances thought, he might as well.

"I want to bring it with me." Everett swayed from foot to foot in the doorway. He was wearing his explorer's shorts and a button-down shirt and a pair of rubber-tipped sneakers. "Mom says I have to get packed. If I bring it to Oregon I'll be able to see you with it."

Frances felt a pain like a narrow wire in her heart. She had been furious with Everett at first. She had taken him out in the yard where their mother couldn't hear them and then given him a thorough shaking: How dare he agree to go? What was he thinking? Hadn't she warned him about agreeing to go to Oregon? Everett had immediately burst into tears: *I didn't know, Frances. I didn't. I want you to come*. "You won't be able to see me through a telescope from Oregon," Frances told him.

"Why not?"

Frances noticed that his shirt was buttoned wrong. "It's too far," she said. "And there are too many things in the way. Mountains and buildings and trees and people."

"I'll climb to the top of a tree," Everett said. "Then I'll look."

Frances was about to tell him that it wouldn't work. But why bother? "All right. You climb a tree, and I'll climb one, too, and then you'll look through the telescope to see if you can find me."

"You can wave to her," Agnes said. She rolled over and began madly waving her arms and legs.

Ordinarily Everett would have smiled. Frances knew he liked Agnes. But now he just nodded and looked at his feet.

"It's okay, Everett," Frances said. "I'll be waving, too."

After Everett went back to his room, Frances shoved her laundry and books and shoes into a heap in her closet, and then she and Agnes went outdoors. Now that school was over for the summer, almost every tree in Whitman seemed to be in bloom. The entire world was green, Frances thought. It looked almost artificial. She and Agnes walked out of the little circle of homes where

Frances lived, toward the wider neighborhoods beyond. "I wish I lived on your block," Frances said. The street she lived on—Albion Street—was a little dead end full of Whitman's newest houses. They were all the same: one-story split ranch homes with attached garages. They were supposed to be cozy, her mother said. The houses were sturdy and not expensive. But what a stupid idea, Frances thought, to build twenty-six houses all alike, as if the people inside them should all be the same.

Agnes' house was on one of Whitman's oldest blocks. The McGuires lived in a two-story white clapboard with a sort of wooden frill around the edges. There was a gingerbread quality to the house that Frances found comforting.

"What do you want to do?" Agnes asked. She whistled for Oops, who wagged slowly toward them across the lawn, like a low-lying cloud. "Should we run through the sprinkler?"

"No." Frances felt too old for sprinklers.

"We could have a picnic."

"I'm not hungry. Can we watch TV?"

"Probably not," Agnes said. "My mom thinks kids are supposed to be kept outdoors, like plants." She lifted the flaps of the dog's hairy ears to look for ticks. "Want to go to the creek?"

"No."

"How about the pool?"

"It's too cold."

"All right, then." Agnes patted the dog and stood up. "I

guess there's nothing else left. We'll have to go spy on your aunt Blue."

Frances didn't particularly want to spy on the person she was going to be living with all summer, but she hadn't come up with any other suggestions, and Agnes was already wheeling her bike out of the garage.

"Come on, hurry up," she said. "Before my parents discover we're here and decide there's something useful we should be doing."

Frances climbed onto the torn vinyl seat. Riding double was something their parents had forbidden them to do. Agnes stood up on the pedals in front, Frances holding her skinny hips as they went up and down.

They rode through the center of Whitman, past the firehouse, the library, and Zim's Ice Cream, and along the edge of the golf course, a fenced-in grassy kingdom where people under the age of sixteen were not allowed. Finally, a quarter mile from the green sign that said WHITMAN, OHIO, POP. 4116, they reached the graveyard that butted up against the back of Blue's house. Frances and Agnes often went there in the summer, because it was easy to spend a few quiet hours among the headstones and not be found.

Blue's house was old, but it wasn't pretty like the McGuires'. It used to be a caretaker's cottage, but it had caught fire about twenty years earlier, and then the caretaker moved away. Now the graveyard was cared for by the town of Whitman, its grass cut weekly by a seventeen-year-old with a rider mower, and the caretaker's house, partly rebuilt, belonged to Blue.

Probably no one else wanted it, Frances thought. Who would want to live between the woods and the graveyard at the edge of town?

They stashed the bike beside the graveyard wall and cut through the part of the cemetery where the oldest stones were, the section they liked best because it made them sad. It was full of narrow white and gray monuments that were sinking unevenly into the ground, reminding Frances of an old man's teeth. It also contained a lot of tiny stones that marked the graves of babies and children. One cluster held the graves of an entire family: Mary, age eight; Eliza, six; Thomas, five; William, nine months. They had all died of scarlet fever.

Frances and Agnes walked upright through the stones without trying to hide. They were too old for spying, Frances thought. Still, she was quiet as she held the metal gate open for Agnes, and neither of them spoke as they approached the bank of windows at the back of Blue's house. Instead of peering in, they sat on the ground and leaned against the redbrick wall. The long weeds tickled the backs of Frances' legs.

"It might not be bad staying here," Agnes whispered. "It's quiet. You can do a lot of exploring."

Frances whispered back: "You mean I can spend all my time riding my bike into town."

"I'll come out and visit you." Agnes looked down at her pale white legs. They were speckled with scabs; she always picked at her mosquito bites. "What's your aunt like, anyway?"

"Strange. She's kind of a hermit," Frances said. "She doesn't talk to very many people. She and my mom don't get along. Blue only shows up when my mom goes out. She brings us donuts."

"It could be worse. She could bring you onions."

Frances snorted. "Why would she bring us onions?"

"She wouldn't. That's why she's probably a nice person. She must really like you, to show up with donuts when she knows her own sister doesn't want her in the house."

"I guess." Frances hadn't thought about the fact that Blue went to some trouble to come and see them. She and Everett didn't have any other relatives. Certainly none that came to visit.

"What does she do?" Agnes asked. "I mean, for money?"

Frances thought she heard a noise behind them, inside the house. She waited, then said, "She does something with computers. She's supposed to be some kind of genius."

"I wouldn't want to be a genius," Agnes said. "Maybe it's better to be just a little on the stupid side, like me."

"You aren't stupid." Frances put a blade of grass between her teeth. She pictured her mother and Everett packing, her mother getting out the vacuum and the rags to clean the house. She always cleaned before they went away, which made no sense at all to Frances. Why not leave the cleaning for when you got back? "Remember when you used to be afraid of the graveyard?" she asked. "You used to keep your fingers crossed every time we walked through it."

"That was for luck," Agnes said. "That was so I wouldn't die and be buried here." She pulled up a clump of weeds. "I remember the first time we came here, I thought you wanted to visit your father's grave."

"What?" Frances spit out the grass she'd been chewing on. It landed on her leg, slimy and green. "My father isn't buried here," she said. "I mean, he isn't buried, period. He was cremated. You know, burned." She looked up at the sky. It was an unreal blue, flat and wide and without a single scrap of cloud.

"Why wasn't he buried?" Agnes asked. "You like the graveyard. And it's so close."

Frances shrugged. She had asked her mother the same question once, but didn't get much of an answer.

"That way you could visit the grave and put flowers on it."

"Well, he isn't buried," Frances said, feeling annoyed. "I don't even know where his ashes are."

"They're in a box," a voice said. "Up in Anna-Louise's closet."

Agnes nearly jumped into Frances' lap. It was as if the house itself had spoken.

Frances looked up. Her aunt's face was several feet above them, framed in the window. "You were listening."

Frances' heart was pounding, but she was calm enough to feel insulted. "You were eavesdropping."

"You're having a conversation three feet away from my desk. I'm trying to work. I do live here."

"What did you say about my father's ashes?"

Blue poked her head a bit farther out the window. She looked like a gargoyle. "They're in a box. In your mother's closet. I saw her put them there after his service. And knowing Anna-Louise, they're still up there." Blue cocked her head. "I wonder why she didn't tell you."

Frances was imagining her father's bones in a box in the bedroom closet. Everett had had a plastic skeleton once, and before he lost the rib cage he had loved taking it apart and putting it together. Blue and Agnes were both staring at her. "She probably did tell me," Frances said. "I probably forgot. I've been busy."

"You look like you have a full schedule on your hands, all right," Blue said. She pulled her head back through the window, then poked it out again. "Do you two want to come in here out of the sun? Or do you want to keep talking about me out there where I can hear you?"

Agnes jerked her head toward the house. "Want to?" she mouthed.

"No," Frances mouthed back, but Agnes was already dusting off her shorts on her way to the door. Slowly, heavily, Frances followed.

"In here!" Blue yelled. The back-porch door led directly into the kitchen, where dirty dishes were piled high along the counters and in the sink. It was even worse than Frances remembered. The linoleum floor was chipped and spattered, the walls badly in need of paint. Past the kitchen was a dining room no one could eat in. The space under the chandelier was full of newspaper and cardboard boxes overflowing with junk. To the left of the kitchen, down a narrow hall, was a rectangular room filled with two large, flat tables. The tables were actually doors, Frances noticed. They were laid across several short file cabinets to form a flat surface. Oddly, the doorknobs were still attached. On top of the sideways doors were three computers, all of them running. On the floor—it was hard even to see the floor, or to know where to step in all the clutter—were other computer parts and pieces, as if a number of machines had been dissected.

"It's not much like your mom's house," Agnes whispered.

"No." Frances thought about her mother nagging her to clean her room. Was she afraid that Frances would grow up to have a house like this?

Blue was typing at one of the computers, the screen casting a glow across her face. Maybe that's why people called her Blue, Frances thought. "Why do you have three computers?"

"It's nice to see you also," Blue said, without turning around. "So, who's your friend?"

"Agnes."

Blue was still typing. "Hello, Agnes. I have three computers because I use them for different projects, in different ways. The ones on the floor are broken. People throw things out. I use the parts."

Frances looked around the long, narrow room. On the windowsill she saw a row of school photos of herself and Everett (had her mother sent them?), and several dead plants in orange pots. There was a single bed against one wall, but it was covered with machinery—cords and wires, keyboards and speakers, broken printers. "Where do you sleep?" she finally asked.

"Usually in bed, though sometimes I sleep right here at my desk. It depends. I've slept in the kitchen. But I do have all the amenities upstairs: a bed and sheets and pillows. Even a new mattress. Go take a look. You'll be staying up there."

Frances didn't want to take a look. "So this is what you do all day? Fix computers?"

"No. Most of the time I fix problems with other peoples' programs. Not in person. I work from here. And I consult with people about the way they set up their systems. I tell them how to do things more efficiently. I save them money, and that allows them to give some of that money to me."

"I wouldn't mind looking around upstairs. If that's all right." Agnes backed out of the computer room into the hall. She probably wasn't sure what to call Blue, Frances thought. *Ms. Fahey? Miss Blue?*

"Fine with me." Blue glanced at Frances. "You don't want to go with her?"

"No." Frances shook her head. "I'm moving in in a couple of days."

"That's right," Blue said.

"My mom and Everett are cleaning the house." Frances picked up one of the photographs of herself, a second-grade picture in which she was missing a lot of teeth. "Why didn't we have my father buried?" she asked.

Blue stopped typing.

"I'm just wondering," Frances said. "We could have had him buried right here in the graveyard. That might have been what he really wanted."

Blue was still facing the screen, but her hands were quiet on the keyboard. "You'll have to ask Anna-Louise about that. Maybe when the two of you have more time."

Frances put down the photograph and pushed her finger into the dirt around one of the plants, its leaves brown and brittle. "You don't water these much."

"I tend to forget."

"That's one of the things my mother says about you. That you're forgetful."

"She's right."

"And she says you're clumsy."

"True."

"And antisocial."

"Maybe."

"And sometimes mean."

"No. She's wrong about that," Blue said. "But three out of four isn't bad."

"She says you used to make fun of her. When the two of you were in school."

"I might have." Blue turned around. "I'd say cruelties were exchanged in both directions. But looking at the two of us, at your mother and me, who do you suppose was more of a target? Pretty little Anna-Louise, or her older, clumsy, antisocial sister?"

Frances heard Agnes' footsteps overhead. What on earth could she be looking at for so long? "You don't really want me to stay here with you, do you?"

"What makes you say that?"

"It doesn't matter," Frances said. "Even after I move in we won't have to see each other very much. You can do whatever you do all day, and I'll be with Agnes. I'll just come back here at night. You know. To sleep."

"That sounds easy enough," Blue said.

"And if I get stuck somewhere, and I can't get back, like if I get a flat tire on my bike, I can just sleep at Agnes' house. Or if it gets too dark and I'm still in town. I could even sleep at my own house. I'll have a key."

"Is that right? Anna-Louise is giving you a key?"

Frances didn't like the way Blue seemed to stifle a smile. "She hasn't given me one yet. But I'm sure she will."

"I rather doubt that," Blue said.

"What do you mean?" Frances was thinking about the extra key in the kitchen drawer. Most likely it would still be there when she got home.

"I mean the house will have someone in it. She's looking for a tenant."

Frances just stared at her.

"A renter," Blue said. "But I don't know if she's found one yet. I saw the ad."

Agnes was slapping down the stairs. "Hey, Frances! You should see the upstairs. There's a little window— "

"She's renting the house?" Frances asked. "*Our* house? She's renting *my room?*"

Blue nodded. "And for the record," she said, "I'm the one who suggested that you stay here. I assured your mother that she could safely leave you behind."

"Wait," said Agnes. "What's the matter? Where are you going?"

Frances tripped over a cord and nearly fell in the hallway, then ran through the kitchen and onto the porch. She ran through the iron gate and into the graveyard, ignoring Agnes, who was shouting behind her in the doorway of the ugly house.

chapter five

"Frances, be reasonable," her mother said. "I have to rent the house. What else can I do? You can't stay here alone, and I need the money to pay for Mountain Ash. I can't afford two places to live." She was making lasagna—one of Frances' favorite meals. Frances made a mental note not to eat it.

"I guess since you'll be locking me out of the house, I'll just have to roam around on my own all summer," Frances said. "Like those kids, the Mahoneys, who always skip school." Frances had already looked for the extra key in the kitchen drawer but hadn't been able to find it.

"You will *not* be hanging around with the Mahoneys," her mother said. "You have two weeks' worth of camp. And I'm making up a list of summer projects for you. Things you might want to work on. Things to do."

Frances could already imagine what would be on the list: *Control temper. Learn to stop being a slob. Find a way to be smarter.*

"Of course it isn't too late to change your mind," her mother said. "You can still come."

What a nice invitation, Frances thought. She could babysit her brother and a bunch of strangers' kids all summer. Probably without being paid. "I can't," she said.

Her mother rinsed her hands under the faucet. "Why not?"

"Because," Frances said. "You're the one who has to change your mind."

Her mother turned around and put a hand under Frances' chin, so that they were looking at each other eye to eye. Her mother had smooth dark hair that framed her face in a way Frances loved, and her skin was warm and smelled of tangerines. "Frances—"

"Whoever you're renting the house to," Frances interrupted, "they'd better not go in my room. I don't want some weirdo sleeping in my bed and going through my stuff." She pulled away.

Her mother sighed and went back to the lasagna, layering the sauce and cheese and noodles in a pan. "If you don't want someone going through your things, you'll have to pack them up," she said. "I'm going to be storing some boxes in the garage."

"Maybe I'll nail my bedroom door shut," Frances said. She opened the junk drawer to look for a hammer and nails, but pulled the handle too hard, spilling rubber bands and screwdrivers and tape and scissors and scraps of paper all over the floor. She waited for her mother to yell at her, but her mother didn't look angry or even surprised.

She just washed her hands again, then started picking things up. "I *am* going to miss you, Frances," she said.

"Despite the fact that you're trying to make that difficult to do."

Even though Frances had decided not to let the trip to Mountain Ash bother her—it was only one summer, after all—and even though she had watched them pack their suitcases and helped them put their bags and a cooler of food in the back of the car, she had a hard time believing that her mother and Everett were really going to drive away without her.

"Frances, do you have your sandwich?" her mother asked, opening the car door for Everett and making sure that he buckled his seat belt. The three of them had already hugged goodbye.

Frances held up her lunch in its brown paper sack. She was standing on the driveway, holding her bike by the handlebars.

"Blue's waiting for you," her mother said. She got into the car and leaned out the window. "Everett and I will call you from the road."

"Rode the road," Everett said from the backseat.

Frances nodded. She listened to the car's motor humming. She watched her mother put her sunglasses on. Still she wasn't convinced that they were leaving.

"We'll see you on August eighteenth," her mother said. "Wave to us, Frances. We love you." The car backed slowly down the drive and pulled onto the street.

Her mother was waving as she honked the horn, and

Everett, his sandy hair barely showing in the back window, was flailing two of his rubber creatures in her direction.

Frances wanted to wave, but she couldn't lift her arms. They were suddenly heavy, as if stones had been attached to her wrists. Her whole body had been turned into a post driven deep in the ground. She watched the car pause at the stop sign at the top of the street, Everett still waving. Then her mother honked the horn once more and put on the blinker.

"Bye," Frances said, just above a whisper.

The car turned right at the stop sign, and Frances Cressen's family disappeared.

On her first full day of doing whatever she wanted without her mother and Everett, Frances had planned to ride to Zim's ice cream store with Agnes. They were going to bring their bathing suits and towels in their backpacks, and after getting two double cones of mint chocolate chip (Frances was going to throw away her sandwich), they were going to ride to the community pool. But then Agnes called and said that her family had made other plans. "We're going to my grandparents' farm," she said. "Just for the day. We'll be back tomorrow."

"You have to be kidding," Frances said. She noticed that Agnes didn't sound terribly disappointed. "Do you have to go *now*?"

"Can't help it," Agnes told her. "I asked if you could come with us but they said there isn't enough room."

"On a *farm?*"

"No, in the car. We have to bring Oops and a bunch of stuff my grandmother needs."

Frances found it discouraging to have her place in the car taken by a dog.

Now she stood in the middle of the driveway and tried to think of something else to do. Her mother had told her that she needed to be at Blue's by five o'clock. It was ten-fifteen; she had almost seven hours to fill.

She finally loosened her feet from their places on the asphalt and got on her bike. She had asked her mother if they could keep the garage open so that she could get to her bike, the pogo stick, the croquet set, and the stilts. Her mother had said no. She had taken the bike out of the garage and driven the other things to Blue's.

Behind Frances, the house, to which she had *not* been given a key, seemed empty and foreign. Soon someone else would be living in it. Frances put her lunch in her backpack, along with her bathing suit and towel. She wasn't going to think about the empty house, or about her mother's car pulling away. *I'll ride to the Foodmart,* she thought. *I'll get a soda and a bag of chips, and then I'll ride to the pool by myself.*

She put up the kickstand and pounded with her fist on the vinyl seat, which often twisted to the right. She pulled a stone from the front tire. By the time she had ridden to the bottom of the driveway, it had started to rain.

"It's good to know that you have the sense to come in out of it," Blue said. "Eventually, that is."

She hauled Frances' bicycle up onto the porch—she could lift it one-handed—and gave Frances a towel for her hair. "Didn't anyone ever tell you not to go biking in a storm?"

"It wasn't a storm when I started." Frances' clothes were soaked. She rubbed at them uselessly with the towel, then looked around for a sign of the suitcases her mother had delivered the day before. She didn't see them.

"Do you want to see where you're going to sleep? Or are you still trying to avoid it?"

"I don't care where I sleep."

"Fine." Blue left her shivering in the hall and went back to her study.

Frances watched the storm for a little while—the lightning cut through the sky like a jagged piece of glass—then wandered into the kitchen. It was a little cleaner than the last time she'd seen it. The sink was still full of dishes, but the floor and the tabletop were clean. "Aunt Blue? Do you mind if I get something to eat?"

"Go ahead."

Wrapping the towel around her to avoid making puddles on the floor (her mother would have insisted that she change out of her wet clothes and hang them up), she opened the cupboards. Inside the first one was a broken lamp and a case of lightbulbs. The second held a cardboard box full of metal parts. She tried the refrigerator. No lunch meat, no sliced bread or sliced cheese, no peanut butter. No juice or milk.

"Are you finding anything?" Blue called.

"Um," Frances said. She found an apple and several oranges in one of the refrigerator drawers. In the freezer she found a package of waffles and several flashlights. "Can I have a waffle?"

"Sure." While Frances was toasting the waffle—the toaster was an inch deep in blackened crumbs—and hunting for syrup, Blue appeared in the kitchen behind her. "You'll have to tell me what you like to eat," she said. "I don't keep a lot of food around."

"I don't care," Frances said. She examined her aunt's oversized blue jeans and flannel shirt. The shirt had a hole in the sleeve about four inches long. "Why do you wear those kind of clothes?"

"What kind of clothes?" Blue looked down.

"Well, loose. Loose clothes. And they look kind of old."

"They *are* old," Blue said. "I wear them because they're comfortable. They were in the closet."

"Where are the plates?" Frances noticed that the toaster had turned her waffle into a hard black disk.

Blue picked up the waffle, examined it, then opened the window and hurled it like a Frisbee into the yard. "Squirrels," she said, "will eat almost anything." She toasted two more waffles, then found the syrup (in what

Frances assumed was the broom closet) and two plates. "Our first meal together. If you don't count donuts."

Frances looked down at her waffle and imagined it as a map. If the waffle were the United States, her mother and Everett were only going to be an inch or two away.

"They're probably west of Toledo by now." Blue seemed to have a way of reading her mind. "They'll stop for lunch. A cup of soup and a salad—no dressing—for Anna-Louise. And a burger and fries for Everett."

Frances didn't feel very hungry. Blue leaned over and cut her waffle for her, as if she didn't know how to do it herself.

Frances didn't move.

"Are you going to eat that?" Blue asked.

"What? No. I guess not."

Blue pulled Frances' plate in front of her and ate, finishing off both their lunches.

Outside, it was still raining. An hour in Blue's house felt like an entire day, which meant that the summer, Frances thought, would feel like years. Blue didn't even own a TV. And Frances still didn't want to go upstairs and see the bedroom. She imagined an ancient, creaking bed for Blue, and at the foot of it, a single mattress on the floor. Except when Agnes slept over, Frances had never shared a room.

Blue stacked the plates on top of the tower of dishes already in the sink and then lumbered back to her study. Like a bear, Frances thought. She sat at the table dipping her finger into a puddle of syrup, then remembered that in the very wet front pocket of her shorts she had put her mother and Everett's phone number in Oregon. "Can I use the phone, Aunt Blue?" she yelled.

"It's on the wall in front of you."

Frances unfolded the wet piece of paper, flattened it out, and dialed. She knew that they wouldn't have arrived yet, but she wanted to call.

"Mountain Ash?" The voice on the other end of the line sounded uncertain.

"Um, hello," Frances said, speaking softly so her aunt wouldn't hear. "I'm just calling—I'm wondering—Is Anna-Louise Cressen there?"

"Hold on." There was a click. "Cressen? She's supposed to be here in a couple of days. Let's see. Arrival: June twenty-ninth. Departure . . . I guess that's open."

"What? No, it's not open. It's August fifteenth," Frances said. "Can I leave her a message?"

"Sure. Let me get a pen. Who should I say the message is from? Oh, shoot, this pen isn't working."

Whom, Frances thought. *Whom should I say this message is from*. Her mother wouldn't be able to spend an entire summer with people who didn't know the difference between *who* and *whom*. "How long have you been out there?" she asked the woman on the phone. "I mean, at Mountain Ash. I've heard the weather is lousy. It rains all the time."

"No, that's not really true," the woman said. "Anyway, we have mountains. It's very pretty. I live here. Okay, I found a pencil. Can I have your name?"

Frances rubbed her head. It ached. "People live there?" she asked. "I thought it was just a place to visit."

"No. Lots of people live here. Some come for a visit and decide to stay."

"Why would they stay?" Frances leaned against the wall. She didn't feel very well.

"Different reasons," the woman said. "Some people feel it's calmer here. Less stressful. Maybe some are looking for perspective. The ability to see more clearly."

Frances thought about Everett and his telescope. She wound the phone cord around her arm. "Are you near a window?"

The woman coughed. "Right now? I'm not far from one. Hang on. OK. I'm near one now. What can I tell you?"

"What does it look like outside?" Frances asked. "How far can you see?"

"Who are you talking to?" Blue was right behind her. How could someone so large move through the house without making noise?

"What?" Frances hung up. "Nothing. No one. I dialed the number for the time and temperature. The weather."

"You didn't want to look at your watch, I guess," Blue said. "Or look out the window at the rain."

"I wanted to know about the weather tomorrow. When Agnes gets back I want to go to the pool."

"And what did they say?"

"Who?"

"The people you called about the weather."

"Oh. They called it mixed. A mixed forecast. A little of this and a little of that." Frances needed to change the subject. "What are you working on in your study?"

Blue walked back down the hall and Frances followed, shivering a little because she was wet. "Two things, mainly," Blue said. "The first is a project for an auto parts store in Madison, Missouri. I designed a Web page for them and now I'm organizing their online inventory and their accounts. The second is for an organization that tries to find jobs for people with disabilities. I'm doing that one for free."

"What do you mean, free?"

"Free. It's called altruism." Blue sat down in her tattered chair. "Doing something because you believe in it. Not because you're going to get paid. They need my services, they're a good organization, and they don't have money."

"How many of the people you work for are like that? I mean, how many people don't pay you?"

"About half," Blue said. "That's why I work by myself. Anyone else would want to spend more money on a fancy office. But I don't care."

"You could fix this place up a little. It doesn't have to be so ugly."

"Ugly is in the eye of the beholder," Blue said. "If you think it's ugly, though, you're welcome to fix it up. I have a lot of cans of paint in the basement."

"You don't want me to paint the walls," Frances said doubtfully.

"Why not? What else are you going to do for the next ten days until camp starts? I need to work. You need a project. Pick a color." Blue turned back to her computers. "Just paint the hallway first. I'm going to be sleeping in here, and I don't want to be asphyxiated by the smell. And bring some newspaper and a bunch of rags for the drips."

"You aren't sleeping upstairs?" Frances asked.

"That's your room. I'm too old for a bunkmate," Blue said. "I'd just as soon sleep by myself in here."

Frances found twenty-two cans of paint in the basement. She brought five of them up the cobwebbed stairs and pried them open, then asked Blue about the paint at least twice more: Was she sure it was all right? Was she really going to let Frances paint the walls? Did Blue know that she didn't really have any experience with painting?

"Listen, Frances," Blue said. "Do you think you can make this place look any uglier than it is now?"

Frances looked around. "No."

"Good. Now get going."

So Frances started in the hall outside the study, covering the dingy green walls with a pale yellow. But the painting was harder than she had thought it would be. She had a headache and disliked the smell, and when she stepped back from her work, she saw that the green underneath was showing through in splotches. The hallway looked like something from a horror movie.

"You'll probably need a second coat tomorrow," Blue said. "Let it dry. You can try out a different color in here."

"What about the smell?" Frances felt achy and tired and might have called it quits, but the paint cans and the ladder and the newspaper were all set up. Besides, she didn't have anything else to do with her afternoon.

"Just try that wall over there," Blue said. "We'll see how it looks."

While Blue worked at her desk, Frances took down the calendar and the bulletin board and tried out an orangey red near the ceiling. It was bright, and she'd forgotten to stir it. Parts of the wall were much darker than others. "This looks terrible," she said. "To tell you the truth, it makes me feel sick." She was standing on the third rung of the ladder, but felt like she was much higher up.

Blue turned around. The rain had finally stopped, and the late-afternoon sun made the walls look uglier than ever. "I think that color makes you look pale," Blue said. "I think you *are* pale."

"I don't think I can finish this right now." Frances tried to wipe a bead of sweat from the tip of her nose but managed only to slap some orange paint across her forehead.

Blue got up and seemed to lunge toward her. She caught Frances and the wet paintbrush just before they fell off the ladder and hit the ground.

chapter six

An hour later Frances was hanging her head over a bucket. Blue brought her cold washcloths and a plastic cup full of chipped ice. "Do you want me to sit here with you?" she asked.

"No," Frances said, though being sick always made her lonely.

"Do you want something to eat?"

Frances gagged.

"I'll take that as a no." Blue stood up and shuffled around in the attic. She had carried Frances up the stairs. At least the upstairs bedroom wasn't as bad as Frances had expected. It was definitely an attic, but it was free of nails and splinters, and it had obviously been cleaned. And Frances liked the ceiling, because it was low and oddly shaped. It made her feel that she was inside a prism. At one end, there was an enormous closet full of Blue's junk, but at the other end, near the stairs, there were a bed and a nightstand and a dresser. Just above the bed was an eight-sided window, like a stop sign, which threw trembling sunset colors on the wall.

"Here," Blue said, handing Frances a cowbell. "You can ring it if you need me. It's pretty loud."

Frances just looked at the copper bell. The room seemed to spin around her.

"I could read to you," Blue suggested.

When Frances was sick at home her mother read to her—fairy tales or other old stories she had outgrown, picture books that Frances hadn't read in years. But she wasn't going to ask Blue to read her *Cinderella*. "Forget it." She shook her head.

"Well, you know how to find me," Blue said.

Frances closed her eyes. A minute later she heard Blue clumping down the stairs.

When she woke up, it was bright. She felt ridiculous treating her aunt as some sort of butler, but she still felt dizzy, and ringing the bell was definitely easier than getting out of bed and yelling down the steps. She reached for the cowbell and rang it. It was very loud.

"G'morning. What can I get you?" Blue called from the bottom of the steps.

"Toast?" Frances' voice creaked. "With a little butter?"

Several minutes later Blue climbed the stairs without a napkin or a plate—just a piece of warm bread in her hand. "Do you feel any better?" She stood beside the bed, considering Frances as if she were a specimen under a microscope.

"Not really." Frances looked at the toast and tried to

decide whether she could eat it. It was flat and looked sort of soggy. "I feel dizzy when I sit up. What time is it?"

"Almost noon. You slept for fifteen hours."

Frances wiped the hair away from her face. She felt sweaty. "Maybe you should take my temperature."

Blue raised her eyebrows, the toast still resting on her outstretched hand. "I don't have a thermometer."

"You could feel my forehead."

Again the eyebrows, but Blue obliged, putting a surprisingly soft hand against Frances' head. "Warm," she said. "But mine's warm, too. I'd be more worried if you were stiff and cold."

"Do you think we should call a doctor?"

"Do you *need* a doctor?"

Frances gritted her teeth. Who was the adult here? Her mother had entrusted her to Blue, presumably because Blue was responsible. Blue had *told* her mother to leave her behind. "We could wait a few hours, to see how I feel."

Blue nodded. "Anna-Louise called," she said.

Frances sat up, willing the attic walls around her not to spin. "When? Just now?"

"A few hours ago. You were asleep."

"Did you tell her I was sick?"

"No."

"You didn't tell her?"

"I didn't see any reason to. It's her first full day out on the road. She sounded tired."

"I'll call her back." Frances pushed the bucket away

from the bed and dangled her bare feet over the edge. She couldn't imagine staying upright on her way down the stairs. Maybe she could ask Blue to bring her the cordless phone. "Did you get the number?"

"No."

"Why not?"

"Because she's probably been in the car already for at least two hours. Besides, I didn't think you'd want to worry her."

Frances flopped back against the bed. A wave of nausea rose up in her stomach. She closed her eyes and fought it back long enough to say through clenched teeth, "That. Is not. For you. To. Say."

Blue stood by her bed for a few more minutes after dumping the toast in the trash can. "Trying to bring her back now would be a mistake. I don't think you should do it."

Frances refused to answer or open her eyes. When she woke up again, the eight-sided window still flooded with light, her aunt was gone.

She was sick for three days. On the third morning Blue suggested calling Dr. Woodrow, but Frances, out of spite, said she wouldn't see him. She would dwindle away to nothing, refusing all food, until she died.

Late on the third afternoon Blue climbed the stairs with a tray on which she had arranged some crackers, a bowl of noodle soup, and some orange Jell-O. The Jell-O in particular looked very good. "Now you've seen everything I know how to cook," Blue said, and because Frances thought the dizziness might go away if she ate something, she tried the Jell-O. She noticed that the dishes on the tray were neatly arranged and very clean.

"Your friend Agnes stopped by," Blue said. "I told her you had your head deep in a bucket or you'd come out to talk to her. She left you this note." She handed Frances a piece of white notebook paper folded into a triangle. Frances opened it. *Bored and desperate*, it read. *Am being held hostage by a Mrs. McGuire on Canton Street. Please send help soon.*

"She biked over?"

Blue nodded. "She's a good friend to you, to brave a trip through the graveyard and then knock on the door of the ogre. Most people your age wouldn't do it."

Frances sucked a spoonful of Jell-O through her teeth. "Did you finish painting the study?"

"Nope."

"It doesn't bother you? Being half-finished?" She remembered lying on the floor of the study, Blue's rugged face looking down at her, on the wall above them a hideous and uneven blotch of red, as if someone had thrown a whole bushel of tomatoes.

"No. It didn't bother me before. Why should it bother me now? If you want to finish it, you can finish it."

Frances dipped one of the crackers into the Jell-O. "I guess my mom called again."

"Correct."

"What did she say?"

"She said that Nebraska is much larger than it should be. I told her you were sleeping. I said you'd been staying up too late, and now she wants you to go to bed earlier."

"Great," Frances said. She ate half a cracker. "What did you mean when you said that trying to bring her back now wouldn't make any sense?"

"I mean it's too early." Blue opened a drawer in the nightstand next to Frances' bed. She pulled out an atlas and traced a finger over a map of the United States, starting in Ohio, then moving west through Indiana, Illinois, Iowa, Nebraska, Wyoming, Idaho. Her square, blunt finger rested on Oregon. "You don't want her to turn around halfway there just because you're sick. It's going to take her longer than that to figure out that she shouldn't have left."

Frances looked up, surprised. "You think she shouldn't have left?"

"What do you think?" Blue asked.

Frances remembered what the woman at Mountain Ash had said on the phone. *Some people feel it's calmer here*. "I don't know. I guess she needed a vacation." Probably her mother's idea of any vacation began with leaving Frances behind. Frances was a slob. She was too loud. And she had a foul temper: Why would anyone want to bring her along on a trip?

Frances studied the thin red lines dividing the states from each other and wondered what her mother was looking at *right now*, what was in front of her through the windshield of the car. In the glove compartment Frances had hidden a picture of herself. Now she wished she'd put it on the dashboard, in plain sight. "Did the two of you always dislike each other?" she asked.

Now Blue seemed surprised. She sat down in a chair at the foot of the bed.

"It's pretty obvious," Frances said. "I mean, she doesn't say a lot of nice things about you, either. She *does* say that you're smarter than she is."

"I'm not smarter. I'm just better with technology, that's all."

Frances looked around the attic. The walls were faded and dirty. "When did you start not getting along?"

"We were always different." Blue shuffled her feet. They were enormous, and most of the time she kept them hidden in a pair of men's work boots. "Anna-Louise was stubborn. We argued a lot. But one summer when I was about twenty and she was seventeen, we had a particular falling out. A disagreement."

"About what?"

"It doesn't matter."

"Was it a guy?" Agnes always said that when grown-ups didn't want to answer a question, the answer had to do with dating and romance.

"Tell me you haven't been watching soap operas," Blue said.

"Come on, I already figured it out. It was a guy. What was he like?"

Blue sighed. "He was a person who came through town,

and neither of us knew him. I met him and talked to him. I suppose I thought I had a claim on him. I was wrong."

"He left?" Frances tried not to look too interested. She set her Jell-O, now partly melted, on the nightstand.

"Eventually."

"So what did my mother have to do with it?"

"What she had to do with it," Blue said, "was that she was charming."

"Oh." Frances wasn't sure she understood. "So he dated you and then her? But why didn't the two of you make up again after he left and my mother got married?"

"We did make up, to a certain extent. But we hadn't been close to begin with, and it was hard, and we decided to live our separate lives. Ridiculous," Blue said. "But I suppose anyone's life can sound absurd when you summarize it."

The phone rang downstairs.

"If it's my mother, let me talk to her," Frances said.

Blue went down the steps two at a time and then reported that it was a business call. But before she went back to her study with the phone, she paused at the bottom of the stairs. "Go back to sleep," she said. "If Anna-Louise calls, I'll wake you up. I'll clang the pots and pans together."

"You only have one pan. I looked in the kitchen."

"I'll bang it against the wall, then. Or I'll bang it against the side of my head. Go to sleep," she said. "I'll come back up soon."

Frances finally talked to her mother that night, but she didn't tell her that she'd been sick. "How's Everett?" she asked.

"He's asleep," her mother said. "He misses you."

"Did he say so?"

"Not in so many words. But he's very quiet. I think he's used to hearing your voice."

Frances ran her fingernail over a burned spot on the kitchen counter. She couldn't think of much to say. "Camp starts next week. You never bought me any hiking boots."

"That's because I bought you a very good pair of sneakers," her mother said. "We saw the rock museum this afternoon."

"Oh. Great." Frances was waiting for her mother to ask her how she was feeling. Shouldn't a mother simply *sense* when her daughter was sick?

"It was more interesting than I thought it would be," her mother said. "They also had a huge collection of fossils. I think Everett liked it."

Frances sighed. It struck her that her mother sounded cheerful. Being away from Frances had probably made her happier already. "Everett likes everything," she said. "That's why Everett always gets what he wants. Because Everett's so sweet and easygoing."

"Frances, stop."

But Frances couldn't. "It's fine with you if Everett wants to drive all over the country to look at some rocks. But it doesn't matter that I didn't want to rent out the house. Or that I didn't want to stay with Aunt Blue."

"You made a choice," her mother said. "You didn't want to come with us." Frances could hear her take a deep breath. "It's late, Frances. I don't want to talk about this right now," she added.

Stubborn, Frances thought. *My mother is stubborn.*

"Everett and I will both talk to you tomorrow. Do you have the phone number in Oregon? For emergencies?"

"I think so." Frances blushed, remembering that she had already dialed the long-distance number, and that it would appear on Blue's telephone bill. "Tell Everett I miss him," she said.

"I'll tell him. Good night. We miss you, too."

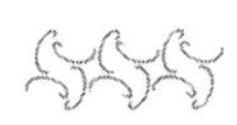

The next morning, Frances felt much better. She ate two plain buttered waffles and threw the burned parts out the window for the squirrels. She stacked her dishes in the pile by the sink, picked up the phone, and called Agnes.

"I feel like I'm dying," Agnes said when Frances asked her whether she wanted to go to the pool. "I can't even lift my head off the pillow. I've got some terrible disease."

"You're sick?" Frances asked. "You can't be sick. I haven't been out of this house since I got here, and now you're telling me I can't come over?"

Agnes groaned.

Frances cradled the phone with her shoulder. "You

probably have what I had. Do you feel like you're going to faint?"

"No. Why?"

"I fainted. It was weird. I had a paintbrush in my hand, and I was standing on a ladder, and the next minute I was on a roller coaster. I saw little exploding flashes. I almost hit the ground."

"I don't want to talk about roller coasters and ladders," Agnes said. "What did you say about a paintbrush?"

"Never mind." Frances told Agnes to call her when she was better. "And hurry up," she said. "Camp starts on Monday." She took a shower and got dressed, and looked for something to do.

Her mother had left her, as promised, a list of summer projects. She thought Frances should read a long list of books for seventh grade. She should practice the clarinet. She should send a series of thank-you notes to her teachers at school. (Who wrote thank-you notes to their teachers? *Dear Mrs. Hatch: Thank you so much for giving me a B- in social studies. Now at last I understand that my research skills are very poor.*) She should take swimming lessons. Take a tennis class. Make a cross-stitch pillow. Frances threw the list away without reading the rest. She wanted to be lazy. In summer, at least, she enjoyed being bored.

Still, there was a difference between being bored at her own house and being bored at Blue's. Frances spent an hour reading the comics and the advice columns and her horoscope (*June is a good time for meeting new people*) and then knocked at the open door of Blue's study. "That paint in the basement," she said. "Could I use it to paint my room—I mean, your bedroom? The attic? Upstairs? I could finish this room later."

Blue didn't even bother to turn around. "It isn't going to make you throw up?"

"No, I'm over that."

"Fine with me, then. Paint away."

Frances opened half a dozen cans with a screwdriver before settling on gold. There was more than half a can of it left, and when she stirred it, she thought of egg yolks, corn on the cob, and melting butter.

She thought that half a can would cover the room, but the walls seemed to soak up the paint as if they were thirsty. If she used two coats, she would have enough paint to cover only one wall.

"Can we buy more of this?" She had called Blue away from her desk to take a look.

"Not of that exact color. I got all that paint at a rummage sale two years ago."

"But you can't have walls that don't match."

Blue just looked at her, her face as expressionless as a rock.

"That would look stupid," Frances said, a streak of paint in her hair. "Wouldn't it? No one has walls that don't match in the same room. Do they? Really?"

She painted the second wall a deep red, the third wall white, the fourth a sea green. She painted until her arms ached, until the shadows on the wall had traveled all the way across the room. By the time she was done, she had paint on her clothes, all over her skin, and in her hair. "I like it," she said. "I don't know why I like it, but I do."

Blue seemed to like it also. The room was strange, she said, but pretty, like the inside of a jewelry box. Frances told Everett about it later that night on the phone. He and their mother had finally arrived at Mountain Ash.

"All different colors?" Everett asked. "Does it look like a kaleidoscope?"

"Sort of. That's a good way of putting it." Frances imagined Everett's face, the way he squinched up his eyes when deep in thought. She wished he could see the attic. She wished she could see his face when he came up the stairs.

"It must look like a fun house," he said.

"It does. Maybe we can stay here together sometime."

Everett didn't answer.

"So what's it like out there?" Frances asked.

"I was sick on the trip," he said. "I threw up in the car."

"I threw up here. Maybe we were throwing up at the same time."

"Then I lost one of my creatures," Everett said. "It fell out the window. Mom couldn't stop."

"Did you see a lot of things while you were driving?"

"It was Rope-Girl," Everett said.

"Maybe I'll try to find you another one. What's your room like? Are you sharing a room with Mom?"

"Our rooms are next to each other," he said. "There's a door between. We already put away our clothes."

"That's good."

"Uhn." Everett didn't sound very sure. "Frannie," he said, calling her by the name he had used when he was little. She had never let anyone but Everett use it. "Why don't you come out here and stay with us?"

"I can't," Frances said. "They don't have a camp out there for kids my age. I have camp here."

"Mom's talking to people in the hallway," Everett said. "They're wearing weird shoes. We got here too late to eat dinner. I hope they let us eat tomorrow."

"Everett?" Frances heard a rustling.

Her mother was on the phone again. "We toured the retreat center, Frances. It looks wonderful. Very homey."

"Everett said he never had dinner today," Frances said. "He's hungry."

"Oh, we're fine. Don't worry. But I need to hang up now. Someone else needs to use the phone."

"You don't have your own phone?" Frances heard Everett introducing himself to someone. "My name is Everett Alan Cressen," he said.

"No, we share a phone here. It's in the hall. I'm hanging up now, Frances. Write to me. Write to Everett. We'll talk to you later." There was a click.

For the rest of the evening Frances thought about Everett, and about the people he was living with, who were wearing weird shoes.

Both Frances and Blue slept downstairs that night in the study, because the paint smell in the attic was too strong.

Blue slept on the single bed; Frances slept on a camping mattress on the floor. She noticed that Blue didn't wear pajamas. She just took off her jeans and her flannel shirt and slept in a T-shirt.

"Everything all right out in the Wild West?" Blue asked.

Frances said yes. Her mother had told her that she would soon begin attending some kind of daily spirituality sessions, and that Everett would look for some boys his age at the Mountain Ash Camp. Though he usually liked to play alone, apparently he had promised that he would try to be sociable. "Aunt Blue?"

"What?"

One of the computer screens was still lit; it was like a night-light in the corner of the room. "Why didn't you keep Everett for the summer, too? Did my mom ever ask you to keep him?"

Blue didn't answer right away. Finally she said, "Anna-Louise might have decided that he was too young."

Frances turned over. She couldn't sleep. "I was wondering," she said. "Do you still think about that guy? The one who caused that fight between you and my mom?"

"It wasn't a fight. But yes, sometimes I do."

"Do you ever see him?"

"Not anymore." Blue gathered her tangled hair into a ponytail. "I used to."

"He came back to visit?"

"No. He lived here. For a while."

"Did I ever meet him?"

There was a pause. "You met him."

Frances thought about the men in town who might have been interested, at one time, in big Blue Fahey, six-foot computer whiz and hermit. "Would I remember him?"

Blue reached over Frances' head to turn off the last computer. "I think so," she said, just as the room went dark. "His name was Paul Cressen. He was your dad."

chapter seven

It was too bad, Frances thought, that there was no erasing things from your memory. She wasn't sure she wanted to know about her father dating her aunt, or about her aunt being jealous when her father fell in love with her mother. She tried not to think about those things. But once an idea crept inside your head, it was in.

Luckily, Blue didn't seem to want to discuss the subject, either. She worked at her desk for most of the weekend, while Frances painted or read or called Agnes to see how she was feeling. "Forty-one hours until camp starts," she said, using the cordless phone so that Blue wouldn't hear her.

"I know," Agnes said. "You called me an hour ago, remember?"

Frances sighed. She was lonely. "Do you know who my aunt dated once?" she asked.

"Your aunt Blue? I mean, no. She dated someone recently?"

"No." Frances squashed a bug with her finger. "You won't guess, so don't bother trying. She dated my dad."

"Your dad?" Agnes paused. "Isn't that illegal?"

"She went out with him before he married my mother. I think my mother stole him away from her. Blue saw him first. Isn't that weird? That's why they don't get along, Blue says." Frances remembered her aunt's voice in the dark: *His name was Paul Cressen.*

"This flu is gross," Agnes told her. "I'm throwing up stuff I never swallowed."

Frances sighed. "But you're getting better," she said. "You'll be better by Monday. Monday morning, right?"

Agnes said she would. "But my mom says she doesn't want you to call so often. You have to wait until at least tomorrow. I'll call you tomorrow if I'm still sick."

"All right." Frances looked at the clock. They agreed to meet on Monday morning, in the parking lot of the Foodmart, to wait for the bus that would take them to camp.

Frances got there early and had to wait almost twenty minutes before Agnes showed up, eating a fried egg on toast while she walked along.

"This is going to be great," Frances said. "Let's get to the sign-up table right away and sign up for rock climbing and canoeing."

"Horseback riding," Agnes said, licking some egg yolk from the back of her hand. "That has to be first."

About twelve other kids, the younger ones with their parents, were trickling into the parking lot, double-checking their backpacks for towels, sunscreen, bathing suits, and hats.

"We should have signed up for four weeks instead of two," Frances said. She had the feeling that her summer—her real summer—was about to start. It was a good thing she wasn't out in the middle of nowhere in Oregon with Everett.

"Uh oh," Agnes said. "It looks like one of your favorite people signed up for our session."

Frances turned around. Making his way toward them was Chip Moran, a boy who had once popped a balloon filled with glue and water in Frances' desk at school. And once, he had chewed up an entire banana and spit out the yellow mess into Frances' favorite pair of gloves. "It's okay. He'll be in the boys' camp," she said.

"Only if they believe him when he says he's human." Agnes finished her egg.

Frances glared at Chip, who ignored her. "We'll only have to see him on the bus," she told Agnes.

Agnes said that the ride to and from camp might seem fairly long.

So that they could be the first ones off the bus, Agnes and Frances sat in front, behind the driver. As soon as the bus pulled in under the red Camp Whitman banner, they ran down the steps and raced to the registration table. They put their names down for horseback riding and canoeing.

"What about rock climbing?" Frances asked the counselor behind the table. The counselor had blond hair in two thin ponytails, and was wearing a tag on her shirt that said *Squirrel.* What kind of name was that?

"We aren't offering rock climbing this year," Squirrel said. "What about sculpture?"

"Sculpture?" Frances squinted at the sign-up sheet. "You mean Play-Doh?"

At the opposite end of the table, Chip and two other boys were signing up for archery. "Hey, this is the girls' table," Agnes told them. "You have to go to the boys' side."

"There is no boys' side, you ostrich," Chip said. "They combined the boys and girls this year."

"What?" The pen slipped out of Frances' hand. "They combined us? Why?"

Several girls pushed ahead of her and signed up on the lists.

"We don't want the boys in our group," Agnes said.

Chip spit on her sneaker.

"Loser," Frances said.

A counselor pulled them all out of line and made them go to the end. By the time Frances and Agnes got back to the front, the only activities left were archery, sculpture, and CPR.

"Maybe we should talk to the camp director," Frances said. She and Agnes had stored their backpacks in a cubby and were headed for archery. Chip and his friend

Wyatt were behind them, deliberately walking through the weeds and brush just off the trail, even though they had all been warned about poison ivy. "Why do those sausage-heads have to be in our group?"

"Just ignore them," Agnes said.

A dead mouse sailed through the trees about two feet in front of them.

"They just want attention." Agnes took hold of Frances' arm.

Archery was awful. Frances didn't see any sense in letting idiots like Chip and Wyatt near any kind of weapon. She and Agnes stood as far away from them as they could. They scratched themselves in the sun for forty minutes while Big Bill, the counselor, gave a lecture about safety. Safety was first. Safety was the most important. What were they never to forget about? Safety. Wyatt guffawed and pretended to shoot Chip with a stick when Big Bill knelt down to tie his shoe.

Sculpture wasn't much better, except that the class was mostly girls. And CPR, Frances thought, was ridiculous. She and Agnes practiced the Heimlich maneuver on each other, Agnes flopping around on the ground and grabbing her throat when it was her turn to pretend to choke.

They ate lunch at the picnic tables and then went to canoeing. Agnes sat in the front of the canoe and yelled, "Right! Left! Rock!" so that Frances could steer. After they tied the canoes to the dock, they changed out of their bathing suits and into their jeans and walked toward the barns for horseback riding. Agnes had found out from one of the counselors that Chip and Wyatt and two other boys were in their class.

"I can't believe this," Frances said, watching Chip cut through the woods again. "I've been looking forward to this forever, and now look what's happened."

"Don't," Agnes said. "You love camp. You shouldn't let them ruin it for you."

"I'm not exactly letting them," Frances said. "They're going to ruin it all by themselves."

Agnes didn't answer. She had spied the horses and was walking toward them. Horses seemed to hypnotize her; she was unable to speak while in their midst.

The riding teacher, Miss Buck, remembered Agnes from camp the year before and immediately assigned her the largest, best-looking horse in the ring. Frances ended up with a dumpy white mare whose sweaty back sagged in the middle. When she climbed up into the saddle, the horse turned around to show her its yellow teeth. Strings of saliva dangled from the corners of its mouth.

Frances ambled around the ring on the horse, trying not to notice the clusters of flies on the animal's head. She dropped the reins to brush a few of them away.

"Franchie! Francine! Excuse me, you! Over there!" Miss Buck was shouting. "Hold on to the reins. And don't let your horse eat while you're riding." Frances' horse was chewing on a dusty-looking clump of grass beside the fence.

Frances yanked on the reins, and the horse looked at her with wild, angry eyeballs. "This horse hates me," Frances said.

"So do the rest of us."

She turned around. It was Wyatt, Chip's friend. He rode past her and grinned.

"Oh, come on," Agnes said on the bus ride home. "He was kidding. And riding is worth it. Wyatt's okay."

"He's friends with that maniac," Frances said, casting a careful glance behind her. "How can they change the whole camp and not let us know?"

"I liked canoeing," Agnes said. "Not as much as riding, but I still liked it."

Frances slumped down on the sticky seat. She was the one who was supposed to love camp. Agnes was there to keep her company. There was no reason for Agnes to be so happy.

The bus let them off in the parking lot of the Foodmart, and Frances unlocked her bike and slowly walked it to Agnes' house. Oops was sprawled like a black and white rug on the McGuires' porch.

"Blaze is a great horse," Agnes said dreamily. "Miss Buck told me that most of the kids can't handle him. She said I was an *elegant* rider."

"I guess it helps to have an elegant horse. I think mine was a donkey," Frances said.

"You shouldn't let her eat so much grass." Agnes took off her shoes and socks and spread her toes.

Inside the house, Mr. McGuire knocked on the screen

door as if asking permission to come outside. "Dinner in twenty minutes," he said, pushing through the door and leaning down to scratch Oops between the ears. "Frances, let me know if you need a ride over to your aunt's house."

Frances knew that this was the polite way of telling her it was time to get going. "That's okay," she said. "I have my bike."

"It's a nice day for biking." Mr. McGuire bobbed his head and went back into the house.

"I don't think you should worry," Agnes told Frances. "Camp will still be fun. See you tomorrow at eight?"

"Sure," Frances said. But she rode back to Blue's feeling hot and tired, and wondering whether camp was going to be any fun at all.

On the bus the next morning she and Agnes sat in the last row together, playing a game that Agnes invented, which involved squatting above the seat without touching anything for as long as possible, while the bus slammed down into the potholes along the road. Usually Agnes won—except for the last time, when she hit her head on the window and got a bloody nose.

They managed to avoid Chip and Wyatt for most of the morning, other than at archery, when Frances noted with satisfaction that both boys had poison ivy rashes up and down their legs.

At noon she and Agnes refilled their water bottles at

the pump and brought their lunches to a picnic table. Chip and Wyatt and a boy named Marty took the table beside them.

"Don't even look at them," Agnes said. "They don't exist."

Frances nodded. She felt sweaty and hot, and the picnic tables were bolted firmly into place in the blazing sun.

She opened the plastic bag she had brought her lunch in. On the last day of school she had lost her favorite zip-up lunch box, and her mother had refused to buy her another. Her lunch consisted of a warm, bruised apple, two unpeeled carrots, a slice of plain bread, and a stick of gum.

"You have to bring your own food every day?" Blue had asked that morning. "Are you sure?"

Now Frances set the food aside and from the bottom of the lunch bag took out a letter she had started writing to Everett. *Dear Everett, How are you? How is Oregon? I'm okay. It's really hot here.* She read the letter over. Sometimes she was amazed at how little meaning words conveyed.

You have to write and tell me all about Mountain Ash, she wrote. *I hope it's not too boring. Are you and Mom okay? Staying at Blue's house is kind of weird. Sometimes I think she—*

The stationery was ripped from beneath her hand. She looked up. Chip was waving her letter around his head like a flag. "Are you writing to your *boyfriend?*" he asked. He climbed up on the table and started reading the letter aloud. His thick, bumpy legs, covered in calamine lotion, were about three inches from Frances' nose. "Dear Ee-verd," he read.

"That's Everett, you idiot," Agnes said, standing up. "He's Frances' brother." She made a leap for the letter, but Chip was too tall.

Frances looked around for one of the counselors. They all seemed to be sleeping in the shade. "Give it back," she said. She was angry but calm. Her mother would be proud of her, she thought, for trying to be so even-tempered.

"So what's the matter with Ee-verd?" Chip asked, still holding the letter. "I heard that he and your mom are pretty strange."

"Oh, be quiet," Agnes said. "Just give her the letter."

"I heard that your mom had to drive Ee-verd to retard camp," Chip said, smirking. "And then she decided to stay there herself."

"Don't be a jerk," Agnes said. "You know that's not true."

Chip thrust the crumpled letter in her face. "What *is* true, then?"

Frances shook her head at Agnes, but it was too late.

"They went to a religious retreat," Agnes said. "But it's not for regular religions. It's out in the woods somewhere, in Oregon."

Frances could feel the climate at the tables change. It was as if the temperature had dropped ten degrees. Even some of the kids who had been quietly eating their lunches looked up with interest.

"Oh, man," Chip said. "You mean they're at one of those places where everyone gets brainwashed? Like a cult?"

Wyatt balled up his lunch and threw it in the trash. "I saw a show like that on TV. They told these people out in the desert that aliens from outer space were coming to get them, and they all dressed up in costumes and took lots of drugs."

"Her brother's seven years old," Agnes said. She was keeping a careful eye on Frances. "He's not taking drugs."

"They probably inject the kids at night," Wyatt said. "With humongous needles."

Frances folded her arms. Something was rising up inside her, something ugly and foul.

"Come on, Frances." Agnes tugged at her. "Let's get away from these jerks."

"That's the way cults are, you know." Chip got down off the table. "They can talk the people who belong to them into anything." He folded the letter and gave it back to Frances. "And I hear your dad is dead, right? They probably look for kids like that."

Frances hadn't realized that she was holding a rock in her hand until she heard it hit the side of Chip's head. He let out a howl, blood quickly blossoming in the roots of his yellow hair. "Help! She's killed me!" he shrieked.

The counselors woke up. Some were running toward Chip, and some toward Frances. One of them pried a second rock from her trembling hand.

In the car on the way home (Blue had to drive out to camp in the middle of the day), Frances was quiet.

"So," Blue said, turning toward her. "A rock."

Frances didn't answer.

"I sent somebody to the hospital once," Blue said. "But I didn't use a rock. I used a pencil." She paused so that Frances could ask her what had happened.

Frances didn't.

"You don't need a weapon," Blue said. "That's the amazing thing. You can drive a pencil right into somebody's shoulder. You can use anything to hurt someone. A book, a shovel, a coffee cup. People damage pretty easily. You can hurt them without even trying very hard."

"He deserved it," Frances said.

Blue stopped at a stop sign. She craned her neck to the right and left, though there were no other cars in sight. "Maybe he did. Lots of people probably deserve to be hit with a rock. But do you want to be the one who does all the throwing? You could spend your whole life collecting rocks."

"You aren't making any sense," Frances said. "I don't care about Chip. And I'm not going back to camp tomorrow."

"I think that's a smart idea," Blue said. "The camp director already asked me to keep you at home."

chapter eight

Agnes called that night and told Frances not to worry. "Chip's fine," she said. "He only needed three stitches. And they didn't shave his head or anything. They just cut his hair really short in one patch. My mom talked to his sister."

"So, your mom knows?" Frances asked.

"Oh. Well. You know, his parents had to come and get him, and they took him to the clinic, and Alison Hardy's mom is a nurse there, and—"

"Okay," Frances said. "I get it. Everyone knows."

"Everyone knows what a jerk he is," Agnes said. "And the important thing is that you'll only have to miss one day. A single day out of two weeks, and then you'll come back. And maybe they'll transfer Chip and Wyatt to another group."

"Maybe," Frances said. But she didn't believe it. She kept hearing a tiny voice in her head saying that camp might as well be over. That Camp Whitman was ruined.

By ten o'clock the next morning, Frances had run out of things she wanted to read. Her stomach was rumbling.

"Aunt Blue," she said, standing in the doorway of the study. "I don't understand how you eat."

Blue looked up from the mess on her desk. "Usually I open my mouth and put something in it, and then I chew and swallow."

"Ha ha." Frances sat down on the single bed. "It's after ten. I've been up for hours. We haven't had breakfast."

"I think I had toast a while ago," Blue said. "But maybe that was last night." Blue didn't seem to believe in set times for eating and sleeping. In front of her on the desk was a pile of licorice jelly beans and a cup of coffee. "Do you want some licorice?"

"No." Out the window, Frances saw a yellow warbler; her mother loved warblers. "I want a meal," she said. "And I don't always want to eat by myself." She had thought Blue was exaggerating when she said that the only things she knew how to cook were Jell-O and canned soup and toast. But she wasn't. Not much. Blue could toast frozen waffles, boil hot dogs, scramble eggs, and make noodles and grilled cheese. And that was it; she had probably been living on these few foods (and frozen dinners) for years. "Maybe tonight we could have a real dinner," Frances said. "Like chicken, or spaghetti and meatballs, or lasagna."

"We can have anything you want," Blue said. "If you're willing to cook it."

"But I don't know how to cook," Frances said.

Blue poured out a cup of coffee and said, "Learn."

After half an hour's search, Frances found a cookbook on a shelf in the basement, behind a box of garden tools. She blew the dust off the top, threw away the jacket, which was moldy, and consulted the index. Some of the recipes didn't look too complicated. Tuna salad. Chocolate brownies. Chicken. Hamburgers. Deviled eggs.

"I need money," she said, walking back into the study and speaking to Blue's broad back.

"How much?"

Frances thought about the things in her mother's kitchen. "I need a baking dish. And some groceries. And maybe a mixer."

"We're having company?"

"Maybe you could just give me a blank check."

Blue hesitated briefly, then gave her two, one for the hardware store and one for the grocery. Frances folded them into her shorts pocket, unlocked her bike, and rode into town.

At the hardware store she bought two aluminum pans, a spatula, a set of beaters, and some wooden spoons. She packed the beaters and the spoons into her backpack and then rode to the Foodmart. Pushing her metal cart through the aisles, she wondered if any of the people in the store had heard about the rock-throwing incident, or about the things Chip and Wyatt had said. Chip had probably told his parents that Frances had attacked him, that she was violent or even insane. Frances shook her head. She wasn't going to think about it.

She started filling her cart with cereal (the sugary kind that she and Everett liked but never ate at home) and bread and peanut butter. Then she headed for the meat department and stopped in front of a row of chicken parts. Which ones did her mother usually buy? What was a *fryer*? Finally Frances chose a package that said *special*, though she didn't know what made it different from the rest. She felt equally confused in front of the potatoes: Why were there so many different kinds? She watched a woman with a baby in her cart pick up an Idaho baker and examine it. What was she looking for? Bruises? Frances turned a potato over. It was the same on the front as it was on the back. She collected half a dozen and a bag of salad mix, then paid and returned to her bike. She hung a plastic bag of groceries from each handlebar, and rode slowly home.

Back at Blue's, Frances discovered that the peeler didn't work, so she had to cut the skin from the potatoes with a knife. (And Blue's knives were dull; Frances tried every single one in the drawer.) There was no salad bowl for the lettuce, so she used plates. At least the chicken was easy. She dumped it into the baking dish and poured a bottle of ketchup on top, then put the whole thing in the oven. She tried to mash the potatoes with the new mixer, but they were too hard and ended up leaping out of the pan in little chunks.

When Blue walked into the kitchen, Frances was out of breath. Why was cooking so hard? Her hair was plastered to her neck with sweat, and the kitchen, all around them, was a mess. Blue reached over and unplugged the mixer. "Maybe you need lessons in how to use that thing," she said. There were slivers of potato all over the counter and along the wall.

"You got some mail," Blue said, handing Frances two postcards. One was from her mother, and the other was from Everett. They were sent from a motel along the route, and they featured pictures of diners and hotel swimming pools and artificial-looking slices of pie. *We saw three deer*, Everett had written on one of them, his handwriting rounded, the letters painstaking and exact.

The postcards struck Frances as old, outdated. Instead of telling her where Everett and her mother were, they told her only where they had been. It was as if her family was living in a different time, separate from Frances, divided from her by an invisible wall. She wondered if communicating with them would be like this all summer: There would be no *now*, only a *then*.

Blue opened the oven and stuck her hand inside. "You might want to turn this on," she said. "Chicken cooks faster if you heat it up."

Frances wasn't listening. She was looking at the postcards and wondering what her mother would think if she knew that Frances had been suspended from summer camp for being unable to control her temper. Most likely she wouldn't even be surprised. This was probably the sort of thing she had gone to Oregon to get away from.

"Good-looking salad," Blue said. She was picking at the lettuce. "Did you buy any dressing?"

"No." Frances picked up a withered leaf and threw it in the sink. What kind of person didn't have a single bottle of salad dressing in the house? She looked at her mother's postcard again. *We're looking forward to the end of the drive and to reaching* Mountain Ash, it said. *I'm sure we'll enjoy the people there.*

What kind of people? Frances wondered. Her mother didn't know any of them. They were strangers.

Blue glanced at the postcard. "Do you think we can eat in about an hour?"

Frances nodded, though the potatoes didn't look like anything she wanted to eat, and she wasn't sure how long it would take for the chicken to be done.

Frances didn't intentionally skip the following day at camp. She woke up a little late and couldn't find her backpack, and by the time she found it, she knew she wouldn't have time to make a lunch. Besides, the kitchen was still a mess from the potato disaster the night before, which meant that Blue might be expecting Frances to clean things up.

Frances sat down at the kitchen table and looked at the clock until it was definitely too late to leave the house.

She pictured Agnes waiting for her in the parking lot, looking behind her while she stepped up into the bus. She imagined Chip and Wyatt clowning around and making jokes about Everett. Frances didn't want to listen to them. She would rather miss camp than have to put up with their stupid pranks.

Leaving her backpack in the kitchen, she went out to the porch and sat on the steps for about an hour. It was hot, but the wind was blowing. The willows were trailing their graceful arms along the ground.

At about nine-thirty, Blue brought her two pieces of toast with peanut butter, and six more cans of paint from the basement, along with some rollers and brushes. Frances waited for her to ask about camp.

Blue didn't ask. "In case you need a project." She held up one of the metal rollers. "Do you know how these work?"

"It's pretty obvious," Frances said.

Blue licked some peanut butter from her fingers. "That's what some people probably say about the electric mixer."

Frances finished her toast and stared at the cans of paint. Because there was nothing else to do, she eventually opened them and looked inside, and by early afternoon she had finished painting Blue's study and was starting on the wooden boards on the back porch floor. She painted a few of the boards a deep blue, then painted the next few red (Everett's favorite color), then gold, then green. She was standing back to admire her multicolored work when she saw Agnes pushing her bike through the long grass at the side of the house. "Hey," Frances called.

At first Agnes didn't answer. She looked hot and aggravated. Her bike wasn't moving very well through the weeds. "Doesn't anybody ever cut this stuff?" she asked. She leaned her bike against a tree.

Frances put down her paintbrush. Her arms and hands were brightly speckled, and her shirt was thick with different colors. She waited to see what Agnes would say about the porch.

But Agnes just flopped down on the steps. She scowled toward the woods that separated Whitman from the neighboring farms. "So. Where were you?"

Frances looked at Agnes' lace-up sneakers and khaki shorts; the legs of the shorts were as stiff and wide as bells. It was fairly obvious where she had been.

"I asked the bus driver to wait for you." Agnes glared. "I made him wait for ten minutes. We got to camp late. Everyone was mad at me."

Aunt Blue leaned out the study window, a pencil clutched between her teeth. Every pencil in the house, Frances had noticed, was bumpy with teeth marks.

"I'd already missed a day," Frances said. "I couldn't find my backpack. Anyway, it doesn't matter. What's the difference?"

Blue pulled her head back through the window, a turtle vanishing into its shell.

"The difference," Agnes said, talking in a strange new

way that allowed Frances to see most of her teeth, "is that I signed up for this camp because we were going to go together. That was the plan. They called your name off the list."

"I don't care about their stupid list," Frances said, surprising herself. "I don't have to go back if I don't want to."

"Why not?"

"Because I don't." She suddenly felt disgusted with Agnes—with her ridiculous shorts and the hurt astonishment on her face.

"I *have* to go," Agnes said. "My parents are going to make me, because I signed up."

"Well, I don't have any parents right now. No one's going to make me."

Agnes lowered her voice. "What are you going to do *here*? Paint the whole house in stupid-looking stripes?"

Frances put the lids back onto the paint cans, stamping on the edges to keep them tight.

"This is because of your mom, isn't it?" Agnes asked. "Because of the things Chip said about her. If you don't come back, everyone's going to think they're true."

"Shut up, Agnes."

"Fine. I'll shut up. I'm going to sit here and get my breath back, and then I'm leaving. I don't care if you go to camp or not. I'm going to ride home and take a bath." She sat down on the wooden steps, but even after she got her breath back, she didn't leave.

Frances touched up one of the boards at the edge of the porch.

"Have you talked to them?" Agnes asked her after a little while. "To your mother and Everett?"

"A couple of times," Frances said. "Not really. They don't have a phone in their room. I don't think Everett likes it out there."

Agnes pulled her hair into a ponytail.

"He lost one of his rubber creatures," Frances said. "I thought about mailing him one, but I don't know where to buy them. I think my mother got them from a catalog."

"He probably didn't bring the whole collection with him," Agnes said. "Didn't he have a big container of them at home?"

Frances stood on the porch steps next to Agnes and looked down at the boards she had painted. Maybe they did look stupid. Agnes was right. She would have to paint the whole porch over. "He did. I mean, he does. But the house is locked. My mother didn't give me a key."

"Maybe you can get in anyway," Agnes said.

"What do you mean?"

"Go get your bike. I have an idea."

They rode back to town, past the graveyard and the golf course, where clusters of brightly dressed people dragged their awkward bags of clubs between pockets of sand.

By the time they got to Frances' house, the sun was beginning to soften above the trees. The house was quiet. The shades were drawn, the garage door closed. A blue Dodge rested in the drive.

"That must be the renter's car," Frances said. "This is too weird, that someone else is living here. I don't even know him."

Agnes stashed their bikes in the bushes. "Come on."

"But what about the renter?" Frances grabbed the sleeve of Agnes' T-shirt. "What are you going to say to him? That you need to get into the house to find a toy for my brother?"

"Don't worry. He isn't home."

"How do you know he isn't home?"

"I just do." Agnes led her toward the rear of the house, past the garage and then under the kitchen window, where Frances' mother used to do the dishes with her back to Frances at the maple table. Frances could picture the backs of her mother's knees, a single blue vein snaking its way down the flesh on each leg. She could hear her mother's voice calling to Everett in the yard.

"Do you know where Everett's stuff would be?" Agnes asked. "Would it still be in his room? Or did your mom pack it?"

Frances didn't answer. She hung back. It was too strange, the idea of breaking into her own house, or worse, being chased away from it by a stranger.

"It's okay. I'll ring the doorbell," Agnes said. "Just to prove to you that he isn't here. If he is here, we'll just say we're selling something. Something disgusting he doesn't want. We'll say we're selling toilet paper."

"Wait!"

But Agnes had already rung the bell. They listened to it chime inside the house.

When the sound died away, Frances felt braver, more determined. She wasn't nervous anymore. The house was hers. She had every right to be inside it. She scanned the windows. The ones that were partially open were covered with screens. Maybe if Frances boosted Agnes onto her shoulders . . .

She turned around to propose this idea to Agnes, but before she could do so, Agnes reached inside her T-shirt and produced a key on a string around her neck.

"Where'd you get that?" Frances stared at her.

"I just got it, that's all."

"Got it where?"

"Shhh." Agnes opened the screen door, which made a creaking noise that Frances had never before realized that she loved, and inserted the key into the lock. With a single nudge, the door opened, and Frances was staring into the back hall.

"Leave the door open," Agnes said. "We can get back outside faster if we need to."

Frances' feet felt like they were glued to the back step. "You first."

In the end they crowded in together, the screen door slapping at their heels.

The house smelled different, Frances thought. Like the inside of an old book. She had never appreciated that the air in her house had a smell.

They walked past the laundry room and the bathroom and cautiously pushed open the door to her mother's room. The curtains and the rug and the bedspread were the same, but all of her mother's things were gone: the bottle of perfume and the lotion and the brush and comb from the dresser, and the photographs of Everett and Frances from the bedside table. In the closet, which was open, Frances saw a dozen men's shirts and a row of men's shoes.

Quickly they walked down the hall to Everett's room. This was even worse, Frances thought. The solar system bedspread and curtains were still there, and so were the stuffed animals on his bed, and the books on his bookshelf. So little of Everett was missing. Other than his clothes and his telescope, he had taken almost nothing with him.

Frances sat down in the middle of the floor and watched Agnes open drawers and search through the closet. She tried to picture Everett shaving his head or being part of a cult. Her mother wouldn't even let him wear cutoffs.

"Hey," Agnes said, backing out of the closet on her hands and knees. "Look what I found." She was holding Fin-Man, who had flippers instead of feet, and Brushly, a silver walrus-like being with a unicorn's horn in the middle of his back. "They were under a shelf back there. Are you all right?"

Frances looked at the toys. If Mountain Ash was some kind of cult, her mother wouldn't have gone there, would she? Frances wondered what Everett was doing at that very moment. Maybe some of the older boys were beating him up. Frances would have protected him at home. But their mother had decided to take him along and leave Frances behind.

"Agnes," she said, holding out her hands for the two little creatures. "Do you think there's something wrong with me?"

"I don't know. Like what?"

"Like—something that would make people dislike me. I have a temper."

"Check," Agnes said.

"And I don't think I'm very good company. I'm not very easy to spend time with. I mean, compared to other people."

"Compared to who?" Agnes looked at her watch. "Do you want to go look around in your room?"

Frances didn't. She didn't want to see her clothes and all her knickknacks rearranged. "Maybe I should have gone with them," she said. "You know, to Oregon."

"What? You don't even like Sunday school," Agnes said. "You're going to spend the whole summer studying religion?"

"But I don't even know if that's what they do there. I never read the stuff my mother gave me." Frances remembered what Chip had told her: *Your dad is dead, right? They probably look for kids like that.*

Agnes glanced at her watch again. "They probably just sit around and read," she said. "We should get going."

Frances hated to leave. Everett's room was so much like Everett.

"Come on." Agnes pulled her to her feet. Together they tiptoed down the hall, Frances' heart pounding. On the back step, Agnes reached inside her shirt for the key again. "I'll lock up."

"Then give me the key," Frances said. "I want to keep it."

"I can't. It's for emergencies. Your mom gave it to my mom, and we only have one. My mom'll notice if it's missing."

"We can make a copy," Frances said.

Agnes pretended not to hear her. "We'll come back," she said. "Some other time. We just can't move anything around."

"When can we come back?" Frances was clutching Everett's creatures, one in each hand.

Agnes wheeled her bike out of the bushes. "I have to go home."

"Can we come back tomorrow?"

"I don't know. *I* have to go to camp again tomorrow." She tucked the key into her shirt. "If you meet me in the parking lot like you're supposed to, maybe we can talk about it then."

Frances didn't get back to Blue's until almost dark. At the edge of the graveyard she saw the glow of the computer screens through the window.

Blue, she realized, was waiting for her without appearing to be waiting. There was a deliberate casualness about her as she turned around in her chair. "What are those?" She immediately focused on the creatures in Frances' hands.

"I'm going to mail them to Everett," Frances said. Her voice was small, just above a whisper.

"Where did you find them?"

"Agnes found them."

"Good for Agnes." Blue tucked her bushy hair behind her ears. "Do you want any dinner?"

Frances had forgotten about dinner.

"I made some soup," Blue said. "I can make you some toast to go with it."

Frances stood in the middle of the room, not moving, Fin-Man and Brushly glued to her fingers. "How long do you think it'll take for these to get to Oregon?"

"Probably three days." Blue stood up. She was so big, so tall.

"I thought it might be even longer," Frances said. "They're out in the country. Or on a mountain, or whatever. They've been gone two weeks."

Blue took hold of Frances' hands and gradually, gently, pried them open. There were half-moon fingernail marks where Frances had been clenching her fingers, making fists. Blue set Everett's two creatures on the table. "Do you want me to wrap these up and address them?"

Frances nodded. "I don't know what it's like out there," she said. "I don't know anything about it."

"We have the pamphlet," Blue said. "There are pictures."

"That's what they show people in their advertising. They probably took those pictures on a nice day. I've hardly talked to my mother at all."

"We could look the place up online," Blue said. "Do you want to?"

Frances sat down. She watched Blue type an address into the computer. A moment later the screen turned a watery gold. *Mountain Ash*, it said, looking like the preview to a movie. Then below, in wavy script: *A Spiritual Retreat Center*.

"So far it looks harmless enough." Blue clicked on *lodging* and then *food*. "Well, they're vegetarians. That's not unexpected. And there's a 'communal work hour' before and after meals."

"Do the kids work, too?" Frances pictured Everett on a three-legged stool, peeling a mountain of potatoes. She pictured him barefoot and in rags, holding out a wooden bowl and pleading for his supper.

"I don't see anything so far. There's no specific link for children."

"What does it say they do all day? What's that?"

Blue clicked on *prayer room* and *schedule*. There weren't many pictures. There was a photo of a woman sitting on a pillow, her legs folded in an impossible position, then a photo of several people standing in a garden. "'Everyone participates in and benefits from the organic and meditation gardens,'" Blue read.

"You mean they do more work."

"I guess it depends on how you look at it."

Frances took the mouse and clicked on *daily reflection*. She read the page it led her to several times, but couldn't make any sense of it. A *reflective soul is a soul that is open. A breathing soul is a soul that is alive*. A *vivid soul* . . .

"Don't look at me," Blue said. "This isn't my area. I'm a technically oriented person. And I prefer my language exact. Nouns and verbs. This isn't something I know much about."

Frances scrolled down the page once more, then pushed the mouse away.

"Maybe if you can pinpoint exactly what you want to know, we can try again," Blue said. "You can think about it for a while, then send in some questions."

"What if they refuse to answer the kind of questions I want to ask? What if they lie?"

"Why would they lie?"

"I don't know," Frances said.

Together they sat in the dark of the study, watching the words *Mountain Ash* billow and sway across the screen.

chapter nine

Back at camp at the end of the week, Frances decided not to care if people avoided her. Chip and Wyatt had dropped horseback riding for orienteering, and they kept to their own table at lunch and to their own section near the front of the bus.

"Good riddance to lousy company," Agnes muttered.

Some of the other kids were keeping their distance, too. Frances ignored them. She knew they were calling her a rock-thrower, a brute. The gossip was that even her own family didn't want her around.

The only part that bothered her was the attitude of the counselors. She could tell that someone had talked to them about her. *Be nice to that Cressen girl*, someone must have told them. *It's an odd situation. Her mother drove away for the summer. Her father's dead, and now she's living with her aunt, the hermit.*

The camp director had smiled at her and welcomed her back. And Miss Buck had praised her just for keeping her horse in the ring.

"What did she think I was going to do, jump him over

the fence?" Frances asked. She and Agnes were getting off the bus. It was late afternoon, but still hot. The parking lot was like a griddle under their feet.

"She was just trying to be nice," Agnes said.

"I don't want them to be nice." Frances watched Agnes unlock her bike from the metal rack. "I want them to be normal."

"Normal?" Agnes put her thumbs in her mouth and a finger in each nostril and pulled. Her nose flattened out like a button mushroom. "What's normal?"

"Oh, quit it," Frances said. "You're spoiling my appetite." She gave Agnes half a candy bar she had bought at the camp store that afternoon.

Agnes tucked the chocolate inside her cheek, then started to drool. "Whoops. Sorry." They got on their bikes. Agnes' parents were going out to dinner that night for their anniversary, so Agnes was going to eat dinner with Frances and Blue.

"I think we're getting pretty good at canoeing," Agnes said. She was pedaling backward next to Frances. "We steered around the buoys today better than anyone else. And we were fast."

"It isn't that hard," Frances said.

"Still, we're good at it." Agnes rang the bell on her handlebar. They turned right onto West Street. "I almost like archery, too. I got a bulls'-eye."

"There's only one more week, anyway," Frances said. "Then camp'll be over."

"You want it to be over?" Agnes looked surprised.

Frances didn't answer. She pedaled hard and pulled ahead, so that they were riding single file.

Because Frances knew that Blue wasn't waiting for them with a home-cooked meal, she and Agnes stopped off at the graveyard and lay down in the shade of the marble monuments.

Frances leaned her head against MARY BOZER, 1874–1940, and dug into her pockets for more candy. She found several warm pieces of gum stuck to their wrappers, and half a dozen rows of sugar dots affixed to white paper.

About fifty yards away, near a row of pine trees, two old women were walking along, one with a cane, and one with a shopping bag and a folding chair.

"That's Mrs. Manderson," Agnes said. "She works at the drugstore. I think the other woman's her sister."

They watched the two white-haired ladies pick their way among the stones. At the foot of a large gray monument, they spread out a blanket on the ground. One woman sat on the blanket, and one perched on the chair.

Agnes held out her hand and Frances gave her several rows of the sugar dots. Agnes stared at them for a minute before nibbling them away from the paper with her teeth. "There's something funny about eating candy in a graveyard," she said.

They watched Mrs. Manderson and her sister put on a pair of wide straw hats. The sister took out a book and began to read.

"Those are poems," Agnes said. "My mom told me they drive out here once a week and take turns reading poetry to their brother. I guess they used to read it together when he was alive."

"I wonder if he notices," Frances said.

Agnes spit out a little piece of paper. "Probably not. But that's the thing about dead people, isn't it? The people they leave behind all get to be sad at the same time, and about the same thing. So at least they get to be sad together. That's what my dad said when his brother died."

Frances studied the older women. The one in the chair was reading to the one on the blanket, who was lying down. She tried to imagine herself and her mother and Everett coming to the graveyard. She tried to imagine them being sad together instead of upset in different parts of the country, about different things.

The wind was blowing. All across the graveyard the grass was bending, moving like a curtain. Frances pulled up a dandelion. She rolled onto her back where the grass was long between the graves, and moved her arms and legs slowly back and forth.

"What are you doing?" Agnes asked.

"I don't know yet." Frances kept moving, flapping like a bird. "Maybe I'm making a grass angel."

Agnes watched for a little while, then lay on her back and made one, too. Carefully they both stood up and looked down at the places where they had lain. The grass flicked back up, one blade at a time, the shapes of their bodies gradually disappearing.

"Grass angels aren't as noticeable as snow angels," Agnes said. "We'll have to remember where we put them."

In the shade of the pine trees, Mrs. Manderson and her sister were laughing together. Some of the poems must have been funny.

Frances swished a wasp away from her head. "If my dad was buried here, my mom and Everett and I could help take care of his grave."

Agnes nodded. "You said he wasn't buried, though."

"He isn't. But if he was, I mean." Frances pictured a headstone for her father's grave. It would say PAUL CRESSEN, in plain tall letters, and instead of a statue of an angel, it would have a carving of a birdhouse and a set of drums. "I think people bury ashes. Don't they?" She turned to Agnes. "I mean, in graveyards?"

"I don't know," Agnes said. She looked uneasy. "Why?"

"Blue said my dad's ashes are up in the closet." Frances looked for the string around Agnes' neck. "You know, in my house. The house my friend Agnes has the key to."

Agnes squinted into the sun. "I don't think I like this conversation," she said. "And I don't have that key anymore."

"What did you do with it?"

"I put it back."

"Put it back where?"

"My mother has it."

"Do you think if I asked your mom for the key, she'd give it to me?" Frances asked.

"You're asking about *my* mother? The warden?" Agnes was digging a hole in the ground with the toe of her sneaker. "Anyway, we can't get back into the house anymore. The renter's always there."

"We got in before," Frances said. "He can't be home every single minute."

"And what if we did get in?" Agnes looked exasperated. "You can't just bury things in a graveyard. People pay for these spots. They're probably expensive."

"Little spots can't be. Maybe we won't tell anyone."

"What's the point of that? You're going to come out here in the middle of the night with fifteen dollars and a shovel? You don't even know what the ashes look like. You've never seen them. You wouldn't know what you were looking for."

Agnes was right. There were plenty of things that Frances hadn't thought of. "I just want to get back in the house," she said. "Maybe we won't bury anything. We'll just look around. But we can ask Blue what the ashes look like."

"You're going to ask her," Agnes said. "Just like that."

"Sure. We'll get her talking about something, and then I'll ask."

"Okay. I'm going to enjoy watching this," Agnes said. She brushed herself off. "Let's go."

While they parked their bikes and hung up their towels on the porch, Frances tried to think of the best way to raise the subject. She was still trying to think of the proper approach when she and Agnes walked into Blue's study, the three computer screens facing them like a trio of judging eyes.

Agnes jammed an elbow into her ribs.

"Uhf. Ow. Aunt Blue," Frances said. "Agnes and I want to ask you something."

Blue glanced over her shoulder. "Oh, dinner," she said. "I guess I forgot. Do you want soup?"

"Okay. Fine," Frances said. "But Agnes and I want to ask you a question."

Blue was already heading into the kitchen. "Ask," she said. She took a can opener and two cans of soup from one of the cabinets.

"We were just wondering . . . ," Frances said. Agnes was leering at her.

"Wondering what?"

"We want to know whether, um . . . Well, can we fix your hair?"

Blue's face, Frances' mother always said, was what polite women in Whitman liked to call *masculine*. She wasn't ugly, exactly, but her face was large. Her forehead was broad, her cheekbones were high, and her nose was crooked, as if it had been broken. But her hair was nice, Frances thought. Or maybe it could be. It was long and dark and bushy, like an overgrown plant. There was gray hair in the mix, but most of it was still dark, almost black.

Agnes looked stunned.

"Fix my hair?" Blue asked. "You aren't planning to cut it, are you?"

"No. But we could trim it if you wanted. Just to even off the split ends. Then we could braid it, or put it up. It's long enough. Do you have a brush?"

At first they worked on her in the kitchen while she read the paper. But Blue said she couldn't read with two people tugging at her head. "This is worse than being mauled by wild dogs," she said.

"Wild boars," Agnes added, running a comb through a tangled section of Blue's hair. "Wild hyenas."

Blue sighed and stood up. "We might as well sit outside on the porch where I can suffer in daylight." She left the soup behind but brought a bag of green beans with her onto the porch. She sat on the top step in the sun, Agnes and Frances on the colorful floorboards on either side. Each of them had a brush and a comb and a cup full of detangler and water.

"Hold still," Frances said. "I can't get these knots out. Don't you ever brush this stuff?"

"No. Ow." Blue reached into the bag of green beans and put several of them into her mouth. "I meant to tell you that Mrs. McGuire called. Something about picking Agnes up at nine-fifteen. Or maybe nine-thirty. I can't remember."

"McGuire?" Agnes asked. "Must have been a wrong number."

"Maybe instead of trimming your hair we'll just braid it," Frances said.

Agnes took a lipstick from her pocket and waved it around behind Blue's head. "Ask her," she mouthed.

"Close your eyes, Aunt Blue," Frances said.

Blue did. A green bean was sticking out from between her lips. But she sputtered and spit it out when Frances applied the lipstick.

"Come on, don't worry. It'll look good. We're just having fun."

Blue let them put on the lipstick—a pinkish red—then let them rub more lipstick on her cheeks for added color.

Frances took a breath. "Aunt Blue, do you remember when you told me about my dad's ashes being in a box?"

Blue didn't answer right away. Her face seemed to register the question. "I remember."

"How do people usually store ashes? I was just wondering."

"In an urn," Blue said. "I should have said they were in an urn. But the urn's in a box."

Agnes went into the house and came back with a hand mirror, a bottle of Frances' perfume, some purple eye shadow, and several hair clips.

"What do urns look like?" Frances asked.

"Why?" Blue opened her eyes.

Frances made her close them again so that they could apply the eye shadow. "I guess they probably look like big jars," Frances said.

Agnes sprayed Blue's neck with perfume.

"No. More like vases." Blue waved her hand in the air and coughed.

The perfume was supposed to smell like fruit, but Frances thought it smelled more like fruit left too long in the sun. "So, my dad's urn looks like a vase," she said. "How big is it? Is it heavy?"

Blue pulled away from one of the hair clips Frances was fastening. "What's this about?"

Frances and Agnes both faced her. Each had been in charge of only one side of Blue's head. Now that Frances saw her from the front, she realized that they'd made her look ridiculous. The makeup was uneven. Its strawberry pink color made Blue look as if she were an overgrown little girl. Her hair didn't look bad, though, Frances thought.

Noticing their startled expressions, Blue picked up the mirror. She looked at herself for a long moment, then took out the clips and wiped the lipstick on her sleeve. "Anna-Louise has done with the ashes what she saw fit." She picked up the bag of green beans. "You'll have to talk to her if you want to know anything more."

Dear Everett, Frances wrote. She was sitting on the porch in the morning sun. The sky above her was flat and still, like a painting of a lake that someone had hung above her head.

You probably feel like you've been in Oregon a long time. Almost three weeks! And you must be tired of eating that cafeteria food. I know how to cook now. I learned how to make French toast.

Frances waggled her pen. She had looked up a recipe

for French toast but hadn't tried to make it. French toast was one of Everett's favorites.

Camp is okay, but not great. Today is Saturday, so I don't have to go. Next summer if you go to Camp Whitman, I'll show you how to protect yourself from all the bullies.

Frances looked at the clock. She had already stamped and addressed the letter. Soon Cliff, the mailman, would squeak along the road in his blue and white truck.

I counted the days until you come home: 31. I hope the people out there aren't too weird. You know what I mean. Are you finding a lot of bugs these days? Write soon.

She signed her name, included a row of X's and O's, and sealed the letter just in time to see Cliff park at the foot of the driveway and shuffle toward her with the mail. Cliff had hair the color of a ripe peach, and the backs of his hands were covered with freckles. "Nice porch," he said when he saw Frances. "I hear you painted it yourself."

Frances handed him the letter. She couldn't tell whether he was joking.

"Package today." He handed her a brown paper parcel that Frances assumed was for Blue. But then she saw the return address: 2240 Mountain Grove, Mountain Ash. No city or state or zip code. She saw her own name, Frances Cressen, on the front. She tore through the wrapping while Cliff whistled his way back to his truck. Inside the package, taped to a white plastic bag, was a note from Everett. *I am not aloud to keep these here bekcaus they are violent. Please keep them for me. There are ten. Love, Everett*

Frances opened the white plastic bag. Everett's creatures, of course. Seaweed-Head. Dumpling-Man. Metalshoes and Silver-Girl. How could a collection of three-inch bendable toys be violent? They couldn't hold weapons. Dumpling-Man didn't even have hands. She searched through the bottom of the bag, then carefully reread Everett's note. It didn't sound like Everett. It sounded like he had written what someone else had told him to write. *Bekcaus they are violent.* Everett was the most peaceful seven-year-old Frances knew. She lined up her brother's rubber toys. Nine of them. *There are ten*, he had said in the letter. He had probably tucked a favorite creature away. He was sending her a message: Number ten he had kept. Even though someone didn't want him to.

"Blue!" Frances took the torn package and the note into her aunt's study, then remembered that Blue had gone into town to look for a part for the computer. Frances felt panic rising up in her throat. What was happening to Everett out there? Why would someone take away his toys? Would he get in trouble when he opened her package, with Fin-Man and Brushly? She ran to the phone and dialed the Mountain Ash number, only to get a recording. *Mountain Ash is a reflective spiritual retreat. . . .* She hung up, thinking about what the boys at camp had said about brainwashing. She remembered the postcards she had gotten from her mother. They were bland and careful: *It's peaceful here. Everett saw a bald eagle.*

Frances couldn't wait for her aunt to get back. She dropped the package and slammed through the door.

"When you need answers or information," her mother had always told her, "there is one place to go." Frances got on her bike and rode as fast as she could past the high school and Zim's Ice Cream, then turned right at the gas station and skidded to a halt in front of the Whitman Free Library. She left her bike in the shade of a tree, wiped her hands on her shorts, and pushed through the heavy double doors, the air-conditioning chilling the skin on her neck.

"I want to read about cults," she said to the librarian, an older man with a sign around his neck that said VOLUNTEER.

"Boats?" he asked. "What kind?"

"Cults," Frances repeated. "You know, religions."

"Ah." He typed at a computer, using only two fingers, then directed her to a corner of the building away from the windows. Most of the books she might want to look at, he said, were on the lowest shelf, near the floor.

Frances sat down, immediately noticing the amount of dust on the metal shelves. Didn't anyone clean the library? She reached for a book called *The Danger of Cults in America: An Illustrated Guide*. The first picture she saw when she opened the volume showed a group of women who had shaved their heads and were each holding some kind of stringed instrument. When she turned the pages, the pictures and stories got much worse. There were cults whose leaders convinced their followers to drink poisoned Kool-Aid. There were cults whose members sold and took drugs. There were groups whose leaders stole all their money, separated parents from children, husbands from wives. There were groups whose leaders threatened their members with guns.

An hour later, Frances noticed a pair of pale legs in stockings close beside her. She followed the legs upward and saw a different librarian watching her through a pair of thick glasses.

"I thought I remembered you," the librarian said. Her name tag said REFERENCE. "I'm Mrs. Voorhees. Caroline Voorhees. I was your Sunday school teacher a few years ago."

Frances was sitting cross-legged on the floor, surrounded by a pile of open books, every one of which contained disaster.

"I suppose you're searching for something specific," Mrs. Voorhees said. "Or you wouldn't be spending a lovely afternoon here in the summer. Can I help you find it?" She looked down at the book on top of the stack. In it was a picture of a group of bearded, barefoot men standing in a circle around a pond.

When Frances didn't answer, Mrs. Voorhees leaned over and closed the book. She closed the entire group of them, then stacked them neatly along the shelf. "I know your mother," she said. "A wonderful woman. Very smart and well organized. I understand she's away for the summer. I don't think these books are going to tell you anything about her."

Frances looked into Mrs. Voorhees' eyes. They were gray, and one of them strayed slightly toward the wall.

Frances remembered her reading a story to the Sunday school class, something about the good Samaritan, then setting out crackers and juice on a little table. "It's called Mountain Ash," Frances said. "Mountain Ash Spiritual Retreat. That's where she went. With my brother. It's out in Oregon, but I don't know very much about it."

"It's a good impulse, to want to learn more," Mrs. Voorhees said. "But you don't want to get overwhelmed with the wrong kind of information. Maybe there's a good reason you haven't found it mentioned here."

Frances nodded, feeling depressed.

"Why don't I try to look it up for you? You can come back in a few days, and I'll let you know what I've found out."

"I'll come back tomorrow."

"We're closed on Sundays. We're closed Monday, too."

"Oh."

"But come back next week. If I'm not here, I'll leave whatever I've found in an envelope at the front desk. I'll put your name on it."

Frances stood up, grateful for the librarian's kindness. "Which Sunday school did you teach? I mean, I remember you, but we went to a lot of different churches."

"I was at the Methodist church. I still am. I just got tired of teaching Sunday school. Too many unruly children. You were polite, though, I remember. I think you attended for several months."

"That was a long time, for us."

Mrs. Voorhees extended a hand, and Frances took it.

She wasn't sure whether they were shaking hands over some agreement, or whether the librarian was trying to steer her toward the door. The older woman's hands were papery and wrinkled. Before Mrs. Voorhees walked back to the information desk, she asked, "If I'm not intruding . . . I wonder what church you belong to now."

"Me?" Frances asked. "I don't belong anywhere right now. I mean, my mom's still sorting all that out."

"Of course," Mrs. Voorhees said. "That's the purpose of religion, isn't it? To make sense of what we can't understand. To try to give our lives a little shape. It's a lifelong struggle."

"It won't be for me," Frances said. "I'm not going to let it take that long."

chapter ten

"Agnes, you have to give me that key," Frances said. "You have to give me the key to my house."

"I can't," Agnes said. They were on their way home, the camp bus thumping its way along the back roads through the dust.

"You have to. I just need to borrow it to make a copy. Then I'll bring it back. If anyone asks me, I'll say you didn't know anything about it."

Some of the younger kids were blowing spitballs. Agnes pulled one out of her hair. "I *won't* know anything about it. Because I don't have it anymore. I had to give it back to my mother."

"Agnes, this is *my house* we're talking about. I'd let you into your house if I had a key."

"We don't even lock my house," Agnes said. "Not unless we go away on vacation."

Frances leaned back against the seat. She felt crabby and tired. Her mother's letters from Mountain Ash were full of happy descriptions of nature. The water in Oregon was so pure! The woods were so clean! The food was so healthful! *I think you'd like it here*, her mother wrote. *I think everyone does*.

Who was "everyone"? Frances wondered. She had read and reread the letter. Was her mother hoping to stay in Oregon forever?

"Don't be mad at me," Agnes said.

The bus rumbled into the parking lot of the Foodmart and squealed to a halt. The kids in front started getting off.

"Want to go to Zim's for an ice cream?" Agnes asked.

"No." Frances got off the bus and unlocked her bike from the rack. The afternoon was hot and windless. The smell of their backpacks, full of wet towels, bathing suits, and sneakers, filled the air around them. Frances wheeled her bike across the street and Agnes followed.

"You're going to the library?" Agnes asked. "Isn't it closed? It says Tuesday through Saturday, nine to four-thirty."

Frances parked her bike again and looked at the clock on the front of the drugstore across the street. It was 4:25. She climbed the steps, Agnes behind her. The library was still open, but when they got to the reference desk, they found that Mrs. Voorhees had gone home. "Hang on a second," said a bored-looking high school student, holding up a large manila envelope. "Is this for you?" he asked, as if he found it hard to believe that anyone would leave something marked "personal" and "important" for Frances. She took the envelope and carried it outside, Agnes dancing along beside her on tippy-toes.

Frances took a breath and opened the envelope. The first thing she saw was a note. *I haven't found much. So far it looks rather nice. Mrs. V.* Attached to the note was a brochure about Mountain Ash, the same one Frances' mother had shown her a month ago.

"What is it?" Agnes asked.

Frances sighed, disgusted. "Nothing." But as she was putting the brochure back into the envelope, she found three additional pieces of paper tucked inside it. All three were copies of articles from the local newspaper, the *Whitman Bell*.

Anna-Louise Fahey to Marry, read the first. There was a black and white picture of her smiling younger mother in a wedding gown. The second clipping showed a photograph of her father. *Paul Cressen, 54, Suffers Fatal Heart Attack*. This picture was grainy, slightly out of focus.

> *Paul Alan Cressen, musician and owner of The Tin Drums, a music store, collapsed in his home on February 17. The cause was a heart attack. Mr. Cressen will be remembered for his lively wit and for his rapport with customers as well as with his music students. He leaves behind a wife, Anna-Louise Cressen, and two young children.*

"Two young children," Frances said. "They don't even mention us by name."

"They probably didn't have enough room," Agnes said,

reading the clipping over Frances' shoulder. "There's probably a lot they couldn't mention."

Of course there was a lot, Frances thought. There were things that she had never known about her father and there were things she knew she had forgotten. But now, with Agnes' chin resting on her shoulder, she began to remember her father's hands. There was a scar across two of the knuckles. The nails were neatly trimmed and flat, with a rim of white. They were wonderful hands, she thought.

"There's one more article," Agnes said.

Frances turned the last piece of paper over. It was small, only one square inch. *Births*, it said at the top. And then below that: *Baby girl, Frances Virginia Cressen, 6 pounds, 9 ounces, born to delighted parents Paul and Anna-Louise. Congratulations to the happy family!*

"Hey, you were in the paper," Agnes said.

Frances stared at the clipping. *Happy family*, it said. She read the clipping again, then folded it carefully and put it back in the envelope with the others. She stood up. "I need that key, Agnes," she said. She didn't just want it because of her father's ashes. There was something else in the house, too; she could feel something waiting for her there. Before Agnes could answer her, she said, "I'm going to ride to your house now. I'm going to invite myself to dinner."

"Frances, wait. I wanted to tell you—"

"It's all right," Frances said. "You don't have to help

me. I'll find the key myself. And I'll put it back," she said, trying to make Agnes feel better. "No one will know."

At dinner Frances made sure to compliment Mrs. McGuire on her cooking. "These are great pork chops," she said. "I never knew pork could taste so good."

Mrs. McGuire laughed. "It's nice to have you, Frances. Would you like another one?"

"No, but I'll take the recipe," Frances said. "My aunt doesn't cook very much, except for taking things out of the freezer."

Agnes was twisting a napkin in her lap, as if wringing water from a sponge.

"More vegetables, Frances?" Mr. McGuire asked.

"No, I'm fine. Thanks a lot. You know, Agnes and I can clear the table and wash the dishes tonight. You've done enough."

"That's a nice idea." Mrs. McGuire stacked the plates and stood up. "I think I'll put my feet up on the couch."

As soon as Agnes' parents left the kitchen, Frances abandoned the dishes and started opening cupboards. Where else but in the kitchen would a person like Mrs. McGuire hide a key?

Agnes was pouting, tossing scraps in a corner for Oops. "Don't ask me where it is," she said, "because I don't know."

Frances lifted up the plastic trays in the silverware drawer.

Agnes reached over and straightened out the drawer, then closed it. "I'll help you look, if you'll just listen to me for a minute," she said. "I want to tell you something."

Frances ignored her. She opened the dishwasher and the refrigerator and the tiny cabinet in front of the sink.

"I'll get you back into the house again," Agnes said. "I'll talk to my mom. I promise. We'll tell her you need to get something out of your room."

Frances pushed past her and opened the broom closet. She was about to close it when she heard a *clink*. She moved the dustpan aside. On a nail, hanging from a string, was the silver key. "Eureka," she whispered.

Agnes didn't even turn around. She was elbow-deep in a sink full of slimy water.

"I have it," Frances said. "Do you want to come with me? Or not?"

"Where are you going?" Mrs. McGuire had come back into the kitchen.

"Nowhere. I finished the dishes." Agnes pulled the plug out of the sink and the water guggled. "We're just going out."

" 'Just out' where? You're going to stand outside on the driveway?"

"No. We'll go for a walk. Around the block."

"All right. But take the dog with you. And on your way you can take these to your cousin." She handed Agnes a pair of sunglasses. "He left them here a few days ago."

Agnes' face turned an agonizing red.

"What cousin?" Frances asked.

Mrs. McGuire looked flustered. "Agnes' second cousin. He's been hired as a summer school teacher."

"Oh," Frances said. "Her cousin."

"I thought you knew. He's the one who's been renting your house," Mrs. McGuire said.

Frances turned slowly, very slowly, toward Agnes. There was a drumming in her ears, as if she'd been holding her breath underwater.

"I suppose I can return the glasses later." Mrs. McGuire looked at Agnes. "There's probably no hurry." She thanked them for doing the dishes and left the room.

Frances wasn't sure how she got out of the kitchen and onto the McGuires' wide front lawn. Her whole body was trembling. Her hands were shaking so badly, she had to make fists in her pockets to keep them still.

"Frances, wait!" Agnes said. "I was going to tell you. I was trying to, but I didn't have a chance."

Frances tried to count, the way her mother did, but the blood was pounding in her head and she only got to four. "You didn't have a chance to tell me that a member of your own family is living in *my house*?"

"I wanted to—"

Oops was barking. They had forgotten him, and he gazed at them mournfully through the screen.

"You're probably in there all the time, aren't you?" Frances shouted. "You probably have dinner over there. You probably hang out in my room and read my books and open my drawers and look at everything I keep private."

"I don't."

Frances felt anger overtake her. She felt like her body might burst into flame. "That day we went in together, I thought you'd stolen the key for *me*. But it wasn't for me. You just took it because you knew where it was. It was always hanging in your kitchen. You just reached up and used it whenever you wanted."

"Frances—"

"You were going into my house all the time and you only let me in it once. I asked you and asked you." Frances was clutching the key in her hand. "Now I can use it whenever I want." She started off across the grass, through the backyards.

"Frances, don't." Agnes trotted behind her. "My mother will kill me."

"Too bad for you." They ran through the Saucedos' backyard and then the Gearys'. Frances didn't stop until she was standing on her own driveway next to a blue-gray car. The garage door was closed.

There, Frances thought. There it was, inside the house. Her old life. Her life with Everett and her mother. She leaned against the garage and pulled on the handle. "Do you have a key to this, too?"

"No."

"Liar." She pulled harder, then kicked at the white-paneled door, leaving a footprint.

"Don't. He'll hear us," Agnes moaned. "We'll come

back tomorrow. I promise. I think I know when he'll be gone."

"I'm sick of hearing about what you know." At the edge of the driveway was a pile of stones Frances' mother used to keep down the weeds in the garden. Frances picked one up and threw it against the garage.

"Frances, please." Agnes was slowly backing away.

"This is for your cousin." Frances threw a second stone, this time breaking one of the windows. She picked up a third stone and then a fourth, managing to break another window before a light went on in the kitchen.

"Stop!" Agnes was crying.

Frances shoved her and ran. Even while she was running, she saw Agnes' face, her shocked and surprised expression, the tears falling down her freckled cheeks like rain.

She ran farther than she had ever run before, past the playground and the tennis courts, the fire station and the school. She didn't stop running until she reached the fence outside the golf course. She ran straight toward it, her lungs burning.

Out of breath, she clutched at the metal diamonds of the fence, holding herself up as she gasped for air. She remembered that, on a very hot night the previous summer, she and Everett had stood at the edge of one of the fairways and watched the sprinklers all come on at once, shooting their geysers of water in every direction. Everett had told her that they looked like fireworks, but without color. It was almost better that way, he said. With real fireworks, you got distracted by the color and sound.

Frances thought about what her mother would say when she heard about the broken windows. Even if she hadn't been thinking about staying in Oregon forever, she probably would now. Who would want to come home to a daughter who was such a troublemaker? A daughter who would actually vandalize her own house? She thought about her mother's letter: *I think you'd like it here*. Maybe Frances had been wrong about Mountain Ash. Wouldn't Mrs. Voorhees have told her if it was dangerous? It was probably some kind of paradise, and now Frances would never see it, because her mother would be furious to learn that Frances was turning into a juvenile delinquent. Her mother would tell her, sadly but sternly, that she was a bad influence on Everett and would have to be sent away to a special school.

Frances wiped her face on her sleeve. She had a blister and her legs were tired. She looked in both directions, then put the toe of her sneaker into one of the metal diamonds that made up the fence. It was easy to climb. She pulled herself up a little higher, then swung a leg over the top and dropped down cautiously inside. The golf course was like a marvelous uninhabited kingdom, the little colored flags of different countries waving between the trees. She took off her shoes and hiked up the slope to the thirteenth green, the short grass cool and delicious beneath her feet.

It was dusk, and her aunt would be waiting for her. What would Frances tell her? During the previous forty-five minutes she had stolen a key from Mrs. McGuire, insulted Agnes, shattered the windows in her own garage, and run three miles in the heat to end up trespassing on private land. Maybe she wouldn't go back to Blue's for a little while.

Frances lay down on the green to think. Something bit her and when she slapped it, she began rolling down a slope toward one of the sand traps. Watching the world tumble over and over, she wondered when the sprinklers would be turned on, the ribbons of water sliding through the air. At the bottom of the hill she dipped her fingers into the sand trap, like a tiny oval desert. Everett, she thought, would love it here.

"Hey!"

It took her a moment to look up. A man was trimming trees near the fifteenth hole. "What are you doing in here? Hey, get out!" He started running toward her.

She grabbed her shoes, tripped, and fell into the sand trap, then scuttled out of it toward the opposite side of the fence. Another man had jumped off a rider mower and was headed in her direction. She could hear him swearing as he ran.

Had Agnes' cousin called the police? Frances took off through the trees, running as fast as she could for the second time that night. She hit the fence hard and began to climb. The two men were shouting at her; one was running toward the gate about a hundred yards away. She straddled the fence and dropped down on the other side, cutting her arm on a sharp piece of wire. She fell to her knees but quickly scrambled up and into a clump of pines. She had lost her shoes as well as the key. The man at the gate was peering into the darkness, but didn't seem to know where she had gone.

Frances waited fifteen minutes, until it was fully dark, then cut through the graveyard on her way to Blue's. "It's me," she called when she stumbled in. "I ate at Agnes' house. I'm tired. I'm going to bed."

Blue's chair creaked once. She seemed to know not to follow Frances to her room.

About an hour later, Frances heard Blue talking to someone on the phone. Her niece? Yes, she had a niece who was almost twelve. The golf course? What about it? As far as she knew, her niece didn't play golf. Quietly Frances turned over in bed, trying not to allow the springs to squeak. She tried to stay awake, to find out whether Blue was going to throw her out of the house. But she was exhausted, and the scenery of dreams was taking shape behind her eyes. She began to dream about her father. He was sitting in a lawn chair in the graveyard, smoking a pipe, though Frances didn't remember seeing him smoke when he was alive. "What are you doing here?" she asked him. In the dream she was only mildly surprised to see him.

"I came back for a visit," her father said. "There are people I've been wanting to talk to."

"Have you wanted to talk to me?"

Her father was looking over her shoulder.

"What is it? What did you want to tell me?" Frances asked. She was trying to get him to focus on her face.

"I want to tell you to get up." It was Blue's voice.

"What?" Frances opened her eyes.

"Come on. We're going out."

"Isn't it early?" Frances looked out the window. The sky was black. "What time is it?"

Blue was a formless shadow beside the bed. "Here are your clothes. I'll be waiting for you out on the porch."

Frances picked her watch up off the dresser and squinted. Three A.M. The image of her father was still glowing at the back of her mind, and she thought about dropping down onto the pillow again, allowing the dream to wash back into her imagination. But the sound of Blue's boots clomping down the steps forced her to put on her jeans and a shirt. By the time she got downstairs, Blue was stepping through the open door into the dark, carrying what looked like a fishing rod.

"Where are we going?" Frances' voice was a whine. Blue's shadow threaded its way through the birch trees up ahead. She was walking away from the graveyard, away from the golf course, into the woods, and away from town. Maybe she had heard about the broken windows. Maybe she was going to lead Frances into the middle of a forest and force her to find her way back on her own, in some weird kind of punishment. Frances followed Blue's dark shape along a rocky path. They walked in silence for a while.

"Here." Blue stopped at last. "Down here." She climbed down into a narrow gully and began doing something with her fishing pole. At her feet was a thick dark stripe that Frances eventually recognized as a stream.

"I think this is the best place."

Frances followed her aunt's voice and carefully picked her way through the brush to sit beside Blue on a fallen tree trunk. Blue untangled the fishing gear, and Frances saw that she had two poles, as well as a plastic container full of worms. She also had a thermos of coffee attached to a strap across her back. She poured some coffee into the thermos lid and handed it to Frances, who sipped. She didn't think she liked coffee, but she was thirsty and tired.

"Fishing is a good way to meditate," Blue said. "It clears your thoughts. Especially at night."

Frances nodded, invisibly, in the dark. The coffee was bitter. She thought she could feel it sending out little electric tentacles through her veins.

"It also makes talking to people easier. You sit next to somebody in the dark, without ever looking them in the face, and you find you can tell them all sorts of things." She handed Frances a pole. "This is the deepest part of the stream. It doesn't look it, but there's a hole down there, and the water's about eight feet deep."

Frances held the pole, her arms as stiff as a mannequin's. She didn't really know how to fish. She didn't like fishing.

Blue poured herself a second cup of coffee. "For example, one person, in the dark, at a stream like this, might tell another one why she came in so late after dinner."

Frances coughed.

"She might be inspired to explain why she left a big smear of blood by the front door and brought half the county after her for her aunt to deal with."

Frances stared at the surface of the water. "I cut through the golf course," she said.

Blue waited.

"I was thinking that Everett would like it. I remembered how he liked to stand there and watch the sprinklers, but we could never go in. So I climbed the fence and lost my shoes and some people chased me, and I cut myself on the way out."

"Was it worth it?" Blue asked. "Being on the golf course?"

"It felt . . . great," Frances said. "At least, for a while."

"Why only a while?"

Frances thought about the windows in the garage. Blue would find out about them one way or another. She felt sick, remembering the rock in her hand, the explosion of glass. Slowly, directing her words toward the stream, she told Blue about sneaking into Everett's room with Agnes, about Agnes' cousin, about the key to the house, and about the broken windows.

Blue reeled in her line. "Luckily, throwing stones at your own house probably isn't quite as illegal as throwing stones at someone else's," she said. "But it doesn't strike me as very smart. Were you trying to get in?"

Frances nodded.

"What for?"

"Because I needed to," Frances said. "Because it's my house. And I was going to look for something."

Blue was quiet.

"I don't think his ashes should just be sitting in a box in a closet," Frances said. "I was going to bury them. Out in the graveyard. That way, we could have a kind of family plot."

Blue sat still for a little while. "You were going to take your father's ashes out of the closet and bury them," she said.

"I might not have buried them." Frances wasn't sure she was making any sense. She was glad it was dark. "At camp everyone was talking about Mountain Ash being some kind of cult. They were talking about people getting hypnotized and turning into zombies and things."

"Zombies," Blue repeated. "And you believed them?"

"Not completely." Frances squirmed. "But my mother left me here, and I don't really know what she and Everett are doing, and I don't think she should have left my father's ashes behind in a box."

Something skittered by in the woods across the stream. "Listen, Frances," Blue said. "There are things that happen in life that a person can't do anything about. There are things we can't plan for, or argue our way out of, or stop. So people take comfort where they can find it. There's probably a reason Anna-Louise still has those ashes up in her closet. What if she came back home and they were gone?"

What if she didn't come back home? Frances thought. But she didn't want to ask that question out loud. She sighed and put her fishing pole down on a rock. All the anger she had felt earlier had shrunk to the size of a clenched fist. Why couldn't she learn to count to one hundred, like her mother? "You're saying I should try to think before I act. I should be more patient."

"It's just a suggestion," Blue said.

Frances nodded. She felt tears begin to force themselves into her eyes. "I'm trying, Aunt Blue," she said. "But I'm a bad person. I do bad things. I'm mean to people. Sometimes I can hardly keep track of who I am."

Blue handed her a wad of tissues. She seemed able to produce almost anything from a pocket. Frances wouldn't have been surprised to see her come up with a well-done steak and a fork and knife. "Tell me how terrible and menacing you are. I'm not talking about crimes against property. Apparently you've been wreaking havoc on garages all over town, but we'll address that later. I'm talking about people. Who have you been mean to?"

Frances blew her nose. "You want a list?"

"Are there so many?" Blue asked. "Let's make it easy. We'll narrow the field and start with the last few days."

Frances thought. There was Chip, but he had teased

her, and anyway that had been a week ago. There was her mother, but of course her mother didn't yet know about all the bad things Frances had done. And Frances didn't want to talk to Blue about her mother, not right now. "Agnes," she said. "I was mean to Agnes."

"And you'd like to fix that," Blue said. "You want to make things right."

Frances sniffled.

"Good. I'll offer you the easiest way of changing a relationship for the better. Communicate. Talk. And if you've been wrong, apologize." Blue screwed the lid on to the thermos. "Apologizing is one of life's greatest skills. Most people don't do it very well. Here, we'll practice. You have to look me in the eye." She turned Frances toward her. "Then you have to say, 'I'm sorry. I was wrong. I hope you'll forgive me.' It doesn't count if you say, 'Sorry if you *thought* I was wrong.' Or, 'Sorry if it *seemed* like I was mean to you.' Try it out."

"This is stupid."

"We can be as stupid as you like. We have all night."

Frances was tired, but she didn't want to walk back to the house by herself in the dark. "All right. 'I'm sorry I was mean to you, Agnes.' How's that?"

"No. You make it sound like you're being punished. Like someone's forcing you to apologize. Try again."

Frances sighed. The log they were sitting on had gotten harder.

"And no sighing. It has to be sincere. Earnest."

"All right, how's this? 'I am terribly, horribly, amazingly

sorry to have hurt your feelings, Agnes McGuire. I was wrong, wrong, wrong, a thousand times wrong.'"

"Nice, but it was a little over the top. And don't forget to look her in the eye."

Frances squashed a bug against her leg. "Aunt Blue, I'm half-asleep out here. I want to go back to bed."

"All right. I'll walk back with you." Blue bagged up the fishing gear and emptied the worms into the water. "I'm glad we didn't catch anything."

"Why?"

"I don't like fish. Do you?"

"No."

"And we don't know how to cook it," Blue said. "Let's go."

chapter eleven

Dear Frances, her mother's letter read.

Camp must be over for you by now. I hope it was wonderful. I hope you were able to go rock climbing.

Frances poured milk over her cereal. Camp was over, but it hadn't been wonderful, and she hadn't climbed any rocks. Her mother should have known that. Frances had already told her about it in a postcard.

I'm going to take some pictures and send them to you so you can see where we're staying, the letter went on. *The lake is beautiful—very cold, and as calm as a mirror. Everett and I went swimming yesterday. He's met a friend, a boy named Henry.*

So Everett had a friend. That was more than Frances could say for herself at that moment. She and Agnes hadn't talked much, and the last few days at camp had been rainy and quiet. Now Agnes had gone back to her grandparents' farm. Mrs. McGuire had sent her. Because of the broken windows and the stolen key, she thought Agnes and Frances should spend some time apart.

Everett lost a tooth, her mother had written. *He misses*

Whitman, but I think he likes the woods out here. At night he uses his telescope.

Frances pictured her brother up in a tree long after dark, the telescope dangling from a strap around his neck.

"What's new in Oregon?" Blue stopped behind Frances and glanced over her shoulder at the letter.

"Nothing, really," Frances said.

Everett and I are both thinking about you. The summer goes so fast! I'm sure you aren't looking forward to the routine of school and lessons.

"She sounds pretty cheerful," Blue said.

Frances nodded. That was the problem. Her mother loved Mountain Ash. For her, the summer was racing by.

> *I'm off on a hike this morning. The woods are incredible. Send news, and keep well.*
>
> *Love, Mom*

Frances read the letter several times while eating her cereal. Her mother didn't say a word about coming home. She and Everett were supposed to start driving in about three weeks.

Frances looked at the calendar on the kitchen wall. It was July twenty-first. Her mother had told her she would be home when—"Oh no," Frances said.

Blue looked up from her morning paper. "Oh no, what?"

"Everett's birthday." Frances checked the calendar

again. "It's this week. July twenty-fifth. I almost forgot. I need to send him something."

"What do you want to send him?"

"I don't know. I haven't thought about it yet. I don't know what he wants." Frances folded up her mother's letter. She couldn't send Everett any more creatures, because he might have to send them back. And she couldn't send him candy, because their mother would just intercept it. "I can't believe I almost forgot his birthday," she said. Maybe that was the plan. Maybe her mother *wanted* Frances to forget about Everett. Maybe they were trying to forget about Frances, too.

Blue leaned back in her chair so that it balanced on two legs. She opened a drawer behind her. "You could send him these." She showed Frances a pad of thick blank postcards, white on each side, and a set of watercolor pencils, about sixty of them, in a metal box.

"You bought these for him," Frances said. She opened and closed the metal box. "He's not even your brother. I think you should send them."

Blue shook her head. "I never paid you for all the painting you've done," she said. "And I think he'd like them better if they came from you."

"I'll say they're from both of us," Frances said.

That afternoon she wrapped up the pencils and the cards, along with twenty stamps she bought with her own money. They were special stamps with pictures of telescopes and the solar system. She imagined Everett drawing pictures on one side of the postcards, then writing her name and address on the other. At the last minute, before she mailed them, she tucked in an envelope full of the baby-sitting money she had been saving. *Maybe you can use this*, she wrote. *I know Mom likes it out there, and you probably both have a lot of friends, but I don't want you to forget about me*. She imagined what Everett's face would look like when he opened the package. He would probably empty out the pencils and keep some kind of forbidden treasure in the metal box.

While Agnes was gone, Frances spent most of her days painting and reading, and organizing things around the house. On Everett's birthday she made a cake, even though she and Blue would be the only ones to eat it. When it was finished—a little lopsided, but heavy with frosting and colored sprinkles—she dialed the number for Mountain Ash, wishing for the hundredth time that Everett and her mother had a phone in their room, preferably with an answering machine. She listened to the distant ringing for at least a minute before someone answered and shouted for Everett.

"Happy birthday," she said when he finally came to the phone. She could hear the clattering of dishes and a bell ringing in the background.

"What?"

"I said happy birthday." She was almost shouting. "Did you get the present Blue and I sent?"

"Oh, yeah." Everett sounded distracted. "Thanks."

Frances explained that the pencils could be dipped in

water, to use as watercolors, and that the postcards could be sent to anyone, even though she had paid for the stamps herself. "Are you having a good birthday? What did you do?"

"We went for a hike. And we did meditations."

"Meditations about what?" She imagined Everett poised on a rock in the middle of a stream.

"It's hard to explain. I got your note."

"Oh. Good. I made you a cake." Frances left out the fact that it was her favorite flavor—chocolate—instead of Everett's.

"Hello, Frances." Her mother had taken the phone away from Everett. "That was very sweet of you. Everett appreciated the markers. All the kids do. How are you doing?"

"Fine. They're pencils, not markers." Frances tried to sound friendly. She tried to sound like the kind of daughter any reasonable parent would want to come home to. But it was hard. "They aren't for all the kids," she said. "They're only for Everett."

"Everything is shared here," her mother said. "How was camp? How are you and Blue getting along?"

"Fine." Frances heard a bell ringing again. "Are you doing something special for his birthday?"

"Of course. We had a song. . . ."

"I mean just you. Just you and Everett."

More bells. "I'm sorry, sweetheart, the phone is right next to the . . . Okay, here. Everett wants to talk to you again. Not too long, Everett."

"It's me again," Everett said. He paused. He had wanted to talk to her, but now he seemed to have nothing to say. "I got your note," he repeated. "I can use what you sent me. You know."

"Good." Frances was confused. "That's what presents are for."

"Yup," Everett said. "You can count on me, Frannie. Really." Even after he hung up, Frances continued holding on to the phone.

The next morning, Frances was tying up bundles of old newspaper when Blue's shadow fell across her hands.

"You have an appointment today," Blue told her.

"An appointment? You mean at the dentist?" Frances didn't want to stop working. She had actually been looking forward to cleaning the dining room and the hall. She had finished painting the study red, and she had cleared eleven boxes of junk out of the dining room. Already Blue's house looked so much better.

"No, with Agnes' cousin," Blue said. "I talked to him yesterday on the phone. I told him you were eager to help him do some work around the yard."

"Oh." Frances tied a knot around a bundle of papers. "Maybe I could go over this afternoon?"

"I told him you were free this morning," Blue said. "You might as well ride your bike over there right now."

Frances hadn't been back to her house since throwing

the stones. When she rode up, she immediately noticed that the grass was long and unkempt. The pieces of wood that someone had nailed across the broken panes in the garage made the house look cheap and ugly. She rested her bike against the lamppost and knocked on the door.

A man quietly appeared behind the screen. He didn't look anything like Agnes: He was small for an adult, and round rather than thin. He had short brown hair and a mustache Frances knew he'd look better without. Overall, he reminded her of a rabbit.

"Hi. I'm the one who broke your windows. Or my windows. Usually I live here," Frances said.

The man paused, then carefully unlatched the screen door. He seemed almost afraid of her.

"I came to offer to do some work for you," she said. "I guess my aunt talked to you about it. And I'm supposed to apologize. I'm apologizing right now, actually, but I guess I'm not doing it very well. Sorry. Anyway, I could cut the lawn for you. It's long. Or I could trim the bushes."

"Do you know how to use the mower?"

Frances was surprised by the sound of his voice. It was very low. Because he was small, she had almost expected him to squeak. "Sure. I use it all the time."

"All right, then," he said. "You can cut the grass." She waited on the driveway while he opened the garage.

The mower was heavy and uncooperative, and Frances was wearing a pair of old work shoes that her mother always made her wear when she cut the lawn. Agnes' cousin, who introduced himself as George, watched her cut the first few rows, then disappeared into the house and left her alone.

It took her more than an hour. By the time she was finished, flecks of grass covered her legs, and sweat dripped down her forehead. She stood on the front steps for a few minutes, reminding herself that she couldn't just open the door and walk in. Finally she rang the bell to tell him she was done.

"Did you put the mower back?" he asked.

"I'd rather you put it back." She kicked some grass off the sidewalk.

"Is there something you don't want to see in there?" George asked, bobbing his rabbity head in the direction of the garage. "Is that why you were throwing stones?"

So Blue hadn't told him about the ashes.

George stepped past her, walked down the sidewalk, and took hold of the mower's black handle. "I'm not used to living in a house," he said. "I grew up in an apartment. A house is more room than I need. And more work than I'm used to."

"Then why aren't you renting an apartment?"

"There aren't very many here in Whitman. And they were all full."

Frances watched him push the mower into the garage. The big door was open, and she could see the boxes neatly stacked and labeled with her mother's handwriting: *Frances, winter clothes. Everett, winter clothes. Extra sheets and blankets.*

"You can come in," George said. "These are your things, after all."

Frances' eyes quickly took in the labeled boxes. She doubted that her mother would write *human remains* on a cardboard label.

"If you tell me what you're looking for, maybe I can help you find it." He was trying to be nice to her. It would be easier, Frances thought, if he were a jerk.

"I guess I'm not sure yet," she said.

George pointed to a pair of garden shears on the wall. "Do you want to trim the bushes? You can show me how. Or you can come back another day when it's not so hot."

"I think I'll come back."

"Suit yourself," George said.

Frances decided that when she came back, she'd get out the sprinkler, too, and water the lawn.

Dear Mom, Frances wrote. She had been trying to write to her mother for several days. *I doubt Oregon is as nice as you say it is. Probably there are parts of it full of bad neighborhoods and nasty people. Maybe you haven't noticed those yet.*

Frances crumpled the letter up. It sounded hostile. She didn't want to sound hostile.

Dear Mom, I'm glad you're having fun at Mountain Ash. It sounds like Everett is having fun, too. Some kids do whatever their parents want, and Everett is probably that kind of kid. I guess you only got one of them.

That was worse than the other letter. Frances crumpled it up. The trash can next to her was full of paper.

"Writing letters looks like hard work, the way you do it," Blue said. She was sitting in front of her computers as if she were a part of the machinery itself.

Frances threw her pencil into the trash can. "Do you always work so much?" she asked.

"I guess I do," Blue said. "Why? Is there something else you think I should be doing?"

"It's not that you *should* be," Frances said. She looked around at the study. She had put the old computer parts in the basement and cleared the last stacks of newspaper out of the dining room and the hall. "I just thought you might want to. Don't you want to go swimming, or play cards, or ride your bike?"

"Not particularly," Blue said. "I don't have a bike."

Frances emptied the trash can in the kitchen and swept up the floor. Because she had spent most of the afternoon cleaning, she had little shreds of newspaper stuck to her hands and feet. Her kneecaps were black. There were twenty-six bags of newspaper and junk on her aunt's front lawn.

"It looks almost elegant around here," Blue said when Frances bustled past with the broom. "I feel like I'm living in a brand-new house. How about some reward for all your effort? Do you want to go out and get a pizza?"

Frances was filthy. She looked around the dining room with its crystal chandelier and its heavy circular wooden table. "Maybe we could stay home and eat in here?"

Blue raised her eyebrows. "You take a shower," she said. "I'll get some food."

Frances showered and changed her clothes. While Blue was gone, she dusted the table and set out the only plates and silverware that matched, and folded two napkins into hatlike shapes beside their places. Even though Blue didn't care about fancy dining, she would probably appreciate a good-looking table. Frances even picked a handful of yellow daisies and arranged them in a jar. As soon as her aunt got back, she called her over to come and look.

Blue was carrying a pizza and two quarts of ice cream into the kitchen, but she peered through the door into the dining room. "Amazing," she said. "It looks like a four-star restaurant. Should I put on a dress?"

"You probably don't own a dress," Frances said.

"That's true; I don't." Blue put the ice cream in the freezer, then headed for the sink, where she scrubbed up to the elbows like a surgeon. She and Frances sat down.

Frances was thinking that it might be nice to say something before the meal, just to make things more homey. At that very moment Blue lifted her drinking glass and spoke:

> *"Here's to the farmer, here's to the land*
> *Here's to the seed sown by hand*
> *Here's to the trucker, the grocer, the cook*
> *May we never forget all the care this meal took."*

"Was that a prayer?" Frances asked.

"You could call it that." Blue put down her glass. "In

case you're wondering, I made it up. Do you like pepperoni?"

"No, but I can pull them off," Frances said. She made a little stack of the pinkish circles on the edge of her plate, then unfolded her napkin and carefully spread it across her lap. "Hey, Aunt Blue? I've been thinking about something."

Blue picked up the stack of pepperoni from Frances' plate and put it on her own. "What's that?"

Frances took a deep breath. "I've been thinking that if my mother wants to stay in Oregon—you know, for good—well, maybe I could live here in Whitman with you."

Blue's hand, holding a slice of pizza, was frozen halfway between her plate and her mouth.

"I don't know what Everett will want to do," Frances went on. "But he has a friend out there now, so maybe he'll stay. I promise I won't get in any more trouble. And if I get on your nerves too much, I could spend the summers with Agnes, and just live with you during the year."

A circle of tomato sauce had landed on the table next to Blue's elbow. "Has Anna-Louise told you that she's not coming home?"

"No," Frances said. "But she doesn't talk about coming home, either." She had never seen her aunt look so surprised. "You don't have to let me know yet. I guess you need time to think it over." She waited.

Blue didn't seem able to think of anything to say. She was still holding her pizza in midair.

"Whatever you decide is fine with me," Frances said. "I

won't be mad at you either way." When Blue still didn't answer, she left her plate and the rest of her dinner on the table and left the room.

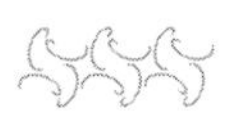

Although it was late and the light was fading, Frances dragged her bike off the porch and rode into town. It was hard to see because she was crying. She rode to Zim's, but couldn't buy an ice cream because she didn't have any money. She wasn't allowed to look for Agnes, who was probably back from her grandparents' farm.

She rode past the high school and the soccer field and the playground, and after a while, almost accidentally, she ended up at 21 Albion Street, and her own front door.

The car wasn't in the driveway, so she leaned her bike against the lamppost, sat down on the cement steps, and looked out at the world. It was after eight-thirty, and lightning bugs were poking their brilliant holes in the cloth of evening. Frances picked up a stick and began to peel it. Out of the corner of her eye she saw Agnes ride by on a scooter. Agnes saw her, too; she waved but didn't stop. Several minutes later she rode by again. Squinting, Frances saw that she had hung a piece of cardboard on a string around her neck. In bright blue letters, the cardboard read, HE ISN'T HOME.

"I know that," Frances called as Agnes whirred by. A minute later Agnes cruised past in the opposite direction. Frances saw her flip the cardboard over. This time it read, MISS YOU.

"Me too," Frances shouted.

"I have to go in," Agnes yelled. "I'll call you."

Frances stood up on the steps and waved.

Just then George pulled up in his car beside the mailbox. "Hello to you, too," he called. He was reaching across the passenger seat to get the mail.

Frances' first thought was that he was stealing their letters. Then she remembered that he was living in their house, and that any letters in the box would be for him. She stood on the step and watched him pull the car into the drive. How could he live in someone else's house, like a turtle in the wrong shell? She looked at the sidewalk, at her tiny handprint next to Everett's in the cement.

"It's kind of late, isn't it?" George asked, getting out of the car. "You should have told me you were coming."

"Why?"

"So I could have opened the garage. For the tools. The clippers. Weren't you going to trim the bushes?"

"Oh. Right," Frances said. Of course it was late. Of course it didn't make sense to do yard work at eight-thirty. "I was just stopping by."

"You weren't throwing any stones this time?" George might have been smiling, but it was hard to tell because of his mustache. "Soaping the windows? Throwing toilet paper into the trees?"

"Not this time." She watched him take a key out of his pocket and put it in the door. "Do you want to hear something strange? Do you know what I wanted to look for in the garage? It was my father. He's dead, but I was looking for his ashes. I thought my mom might have stored them in there."

George stood very still. He studied her for a little while. "Would you like some iced tea?"

Frances nodded.

"I'll get us some." He didn't invite her into the house, but went inside and left her on the step, coming back a few minutes later with iced tea in two of Everett's favorite glasses, the tall, thin kind with a circle of funny faces around the rim.

"So," George said. "I'm sorry to hear about your father."

"Thanks." Frances nodded. "He died a long time ago. I don't remember him very well. My brother doesn't, either. But my mom probably does."

They were sitting side by side on the stoop, the crickets chirring in the bushes.

"Thank you for letting me stay in your house," George said. "I've kept it neat. No wild parties. And now I have help taking care of the lawn."

Frances sipped her tea, tipping the glass so that the sugar on the bottom slid toward her mouth. Lights were going on in the houses across the street. "I don't know if she's said anything to you about it," Frances said, wiping her eyes. "But I think my mom might change her plans. I mean, she might change her mind about when she's coming home."

George looked confused. "She already did change her mind," he said. "She just told me I had to move out by the fifth of August. I thought I had until the seventeenth."

"What?" Frances nearly dropped her iced tea. "When? Did she call you?"

"No. I got a postcard."

"From my mother?"

"Just a second, I'll get it." He went into the house and came back with a small white card. He read it aloud. "I will be back on August fifth. Please move out before then."

"That's all it says?" Frances scratched her head. Why wouldn't her mother have called her?

"That's it." George handed her the card. "Look at that. A stamp of the solar system. And someone painted a picture on the other side."

chapter twelve

"Talk to me," Blue said. "And slow down. Start at the beginning. What are you saying about a postcard?"

Frances gasped. She felt like she was swallowing pockets of air. "Everett," she said. "He sent me a postcard. At the house. It said he was coming home on the fifth."

Blue frowned. "How do you know it was from Everett? If he was sending you a letter, why wouldn't he have sent it to you here?"

"Because he only wanted *me* to see it. He probably thought I was picking up our mail. And he said something on the phone about our counting on each other. I sent him that stamp. And I told him not to forget about me. I think he's leaving Mountain Ash."

Blue paused. "By himself?"

"It was his handwriting," Frances said. "The postcard wasn't from my mother. I *told* you she doesn't want to come back. But Everett does. He told George to move out of the house so that he can come home."

"But how would he get here?"

Frances was already reaching for the phone. She called

Mountain Ash, but no one answered, and she hung up without leaving a message.

"We'll call them in the morning," Blue said, after they'd tried the number a few more times. "Maybe Everett sent that card for another reason."

"What other reason?" Frances asked.

Blue didn't know.

Frances went up to her room, got undressed, and spent a few hours lying in the dark. She should have agreed to go to Oregon. Or she should have insisted, at the beginning of the summer, that their mother go to Mountain Ash by herself, leaving Everett behind with Blue and Frances.

Long after midnight she heard the shower running. Blue was up, or perhaps she had never gone to sleep. Frances got out of bed and went downstairs to use the bathroom. While she waited for Blue to get out of the shower, she was drawn toward the glow of the computer screens. In the upper corner of the center screen was a yellow square that looked familiar. She felt a prickling at the back of her neck and moved closer: *Mountain Ash*. She sat down in Blue's chair, clicked on the yellow box, and saw a series of e-mails. She scrolled up and down and realized that she was looking at messages sent between her mother and her aunt. She started reading near the bottom.

. . . and I hear for the first time today that she thinks you aren't coming back. What on earth have you been telling her? I shouldn't have to remind you that it's your responsibility . . .

Frances heard the shower turn off in the bathroom. She quickly scrolled up.

. . . a wonderful, nurturing environment for children. The art program is far superior to anything I've seen in the public schools in Ohio, and I . . .

Her mother's message rambled on about "tactile experiences" and "cooperative learning." Frances scrolled up the screen. Blue's latest message was written in capital letters.

SHE'S WORRIED ABOUT YOU AND AFRAID FOR EVERETT. YOU HAVE TO TALK TO HER. SHE NEEDS TO TRUST YOU. SHE NEEDS TO KNOW THAT YOU'LL KEEP YOUR WORD.

Frances scrolled up to read her mother's response.

Of course *I'm going to talk to her. Tell her Everett's fine. I just tucked him into bed. Ask Frances to call me tomorrow—I won't be working in the afternoon. Tell her I'm sending her a ticket in the mail.*

A ticket, Frances thought. A plane ticket to Oregon.

"I asked her to check on Everett for you," Blue said behind her, making Frances jump. "But I suppose I worded things a bit strongly, and now she's annoyed. You know how that is."

"You've been e-mailing with her." Frances was stunned. "Why didn't you tell me?"

"I wasn't e-mailing, until a few hours ago. I left a message at the switchboard and all of a sudden there she was, on my computer. I guess they only have one computer out there, in the main office, and she isn't really allowed to use it."

"She said she bought me a ticket to Oregon," Frances said. "She wants to see me?"

Blue sat down, unwrapping a towel from her hair. "Of course she wants to see you."

"She's probably just saying that," Frances said. She hit the X in the corner of the screen, and the messages on the computer disappeared. "Did she say when the ticket is for?"

"Next week. Tuesday morning. I told her she had to buy two."

"She really *does* want to stay there." Frances shook her head. "She wants to leave Whitman."

"I think she wants to consider it," Blue said.

Frances moved the cursor to *check mail* and clicked. Nothing. "Why two tickets?" she asked. "Who's the other one for?"

"Me. I didn't want you to fly alone."

Frances realized that Blue still hadn't answered her question about letting Frances stay with her in Whitman. "I didn't think my mother had money for plane tickets," she said.

Blue shrugged. "She must miss you a lot."

"I don't know about that," Frances said. "I'm not the

kind of person people miss. I'm probably the reason she left in the first place."

Blue looked as if she were about to laugh. With her hair wet and pulled away from her forehead, she reminded Frances of a seal. "She didn't leave because of you," Blue said. "She left because she's Anna-Louise Cressen, and she wants everything to fit and make perfect sense. But sometimes things just don't make sense. People die, and the people they leave behind are lonely."

"You think my mother's lonely?" Frances asked.

"Everyone's lonely," Blue said. "It's what you do with the loneliness that counts."

Frances looked around the cluttered room at the back of the house, with its three computers, its unmade bed, and its bank of windows overlooking the graveyard. Was her aunt Blue lonely? "What do you think I should do?" she asked.

"I think you should talk to her tomorrow. As soon as you're ready. And calmly, if you possibly can. With an open mind."

Frances sat down on Blue's bed, and Blue sat beside her. Her hair smelled of ferns. Through the window, Frances noticed a slender pink line on top of the graveyard wall.

"Sunrise," Blue said as if she'd heard her thoughts.

Inch by inch, the stones in the graveyard were touched by color and light. They seemed almost to come alive.

"I wish Everett could see this," Frances said. She leaned against Blue's shoulder.

The tallest of the gravestones glowed above the wall.

When Frances woke up again, in Blue's single bed, it was ten o'clock. She knew it was ten o'clock because Agnes was standing in front of her, holding a plastic alarm clock in her hand. The two faces, Agnes' and the clock's, seemed to be telling her she had overslept for something. For what?

"My mom's outside," Agnes said. "She's taking us shopping."

Frances sat up and ran a hand through her uncombed hair. Her mouth felt foul, as if each of her teeth were coated in a layer of moss. "I thought your mom didn't want me to see you."

"She didn't. But she changed her mind."

Frances nodded. She remembered the e-mail from the night before, the plane ticket to Oregon. "I'm supposed to call Mountain Ash this afternoon."

"I know," Agnes said. "We'll be back in time. Besides, your aunt says there's no way she's ever going to take us to the mall, so if you need to go shopping before school starts, you'd better go with me."

Frances stumbled into the bathroom to brush her teeth. The inside of her head was still clouded with dreams.

"She told me you might go out to Oregon." Agnes handed Frances a pair of shorts and a T-shirt. "Maybe just for a visit?"

Frances' mouth was foamy with toothpaste.

"Or do you think it'll be more than a visit?" Agnes asked. "I guess your mom likes it a lot out there."

Frances spit into the sink.

"I guess no matter where you live you need school supplies," Agnes said. "That's what my mom says. They probably use pencils and paper out there."

"I'm going to get dressed," Frances said.

"I'll get your sneakers." Agnes handed her a towel. "We'll wait in the car."

Five minutes later Frances was seated in the back of the McGuires' station wagon, the vinyl seat sticking to her legs. They pulled onto the main road before she remembered that she hadn't brought any money.

"It's okay," Agnes said. "Your aunt gave my mom some money for your stuff and said to tell you to buy a lunch box."

Mrs. McGuire looked at Frances in the rearview mirror. "How's your family?" she asked.

It was an ordinary question, Frances thought. Six months earlier she would simply have answered, "Fine." But now she was stumped. What could she say? *My mother left me behind because she's lonely. I think my brother wants to run away. Please don't tell them that I'm a juvenile delinquent.* Frances opened her mouth and then closed it.

Mrs. McGuire barely seemed to notice. "I'm sorry we didn't invite you out to the farm this summer." She smiled.

"That's okay," Frances said. It was a good apology, according to Blue's criteria. Even though she'd had to use the mirror, Mrs. McGuire had looked her straight in the eye.

~

At the store, in addition to a lunch box, Frances bought a new backpack, half a dozen notebooks, and a supply of pencils and pens. The start of a new school year generally gave her hope. All the blank paper and the unopened books hinted at new potential and success. But this year they only seemed to mean uncertainty, a blank future.

Afterward, Mrs. McGuire insisted on buying Frances a purple sweater. She said it complimented the color of her eyes, but Frances knew she was trying to cheer her up. Mrs. McGuire also bought lunch, followed by ice cream, at Burger Heaven. Then she dropped Agnes and Frances off at the end of Blue's gravel drive.

Agnes scuffed up her new sneakers in the dirt as soon as the car was out of sight. "My mom feels bad about not letting me see you," she said. "I asked her how she would feel if I got in trouble while she and my father were away, and my friends were told to turn their backs on me."

Frances tried to imagine the McGuires leaving Agnes behind for a summer. It seemed impossible. Out of character. "I guess it worked," she said.

Agnes was kicking up so much gravel that a cloud of gray dust had risen up around them. "I hope your mom doesn't decide that you should all move out there," she said. "But if she does, maybe you could stay with us—for part of the year at least. Now that my mom feels guilty, she might offer to keep you for a while."

Frances thought about what it would be like to live with the McGuires. There were so many things she liked about their house: the wide front porch with its wooden swing, the triple-decker laundry chute, and the pillows on Agnes' bed that had to be stuffed every morning into fancy cases, like little sausages with ruffles of fabric at the ends. But she didn't belong there. "You might get tired of having me," she said. "It might ruin our friendship. Oops might decide he likes me better than he likes you. Why are you making all that dust?"

Agnes stopped kicking. "I don't know. Maybe because I can stand here and tell you whatever I want. I can tell you that you should stay here. That you should let your mother live in Oregon without you. But I don't know if that makes any sense. If it was my mother, I'd end up going. So maybe I'm saying all the wrong things."

"You never say the wrong things," Frances said. "You're Agnes McGuire."

"Oh, that's right." Agnes sniffed. "I almost forgot."

Frances punched her lightly on the arm, and Agnes responded by squeezing the skin of Frances' wrist with her thumb and finger. Frances shrieked and poked a finger into Agnes' ear. They were still pinching and slapping each other and laughing when they reached the porch.

Blue was on the phone in the doorway. Both girls fell silent when they saw her face.

"It's about Everett," Blue said. "You were right. He's gone."

chapter thirteen

"Gone?" Frances dropped her packages. "What do you mean, gone? I don't know what that means."

Blue's face was pale. "He seems to be missing," she said. "Anna-Louise called half an hour ago."

Frances looked at her watch. It was four-thirty. That meant one-thirty in Oregon. "Where's the phone?" She pushed through the screen door into the kitchen. She needed to call Mountain Ash. Then she needed to call the police and the FBI.

"First of all, sit down," Blue said, catching Frances by the back of the shirt and depositing her, weak-legged, in a chair. "Your mother already called the police, and so did I. Agnes, would you please get her a cup of water?"

Agnes filled a cup at the sink. Her hands were shaking so much that most of the water ended up on the counter and the floor. She handed the remainder of it to Frances.

"She sent you the e-mail," Frances said. "You asked her to check on him last night."

"She did check on him, around midnight. He was

asleep in bed. But she found out that he was missing this afternoon."

Frances felt sick. She listened to Blue explaining that her mother had gotten up early to work in the kitchen and left a note for Everett to meet her at breakfast. He didn't show up, but his friend Henry said that he and Everett had eaten a picnic breakfast in his room. "Anna-Louise didn't get suspicious until just before lunch," Blue said. "She went to look for him and couldn't find him, so she cornered Henry and he confessed. Everett paid him five dollars to lie about the picnic breakfast." Blue sighed. "They think he snuck out of the building at around one A.M."

"In the dark," Frances said. "Where did he go?"

"They don't know yet. People are looking for him now. The Oregon police think he might have walked or even hitchhiked into town, then tried to get on a train or a bus."

"Who would pick up an eight-year-old hitchhiker?" Frances asked. As soon as the words were out of her mouth, she knew. People who did terrible things to children. People who kidnapped them or sold them, so that the children's faces ended up on flyers all over the country. *Age-enhanced*, the flyers often said, showing photos of the people as they would look years later. What would Everett's face look like on a flyer? What would he look like in several years? Frances leaned over and put her head between her knees.

"But where would Everett get the money for a train or a bus?" Agnes asked.

Frances looked up. "Oh."

"What do you mean, 'Oh'?" Blue squatted beside her. "Frances? You sent him money? How much?"

"I sent it with his birthday presents," Frances said. "I felt bad because the presents were really from you, and I wanted to send him something of my own. It was my baby-sitting money." She paused. "Fifty-five dollars."

"All right," Blue said. "Now we can try to figure out how far he can get for fifty-five bucks."

"Fifty," Agnes said. "He spent five already, on that other boy."

"Fifty, then." Blue picked up the phone and began to dial.

"Ms. Fahey?" A police officer was standing at the open door. Frances looked at his face and then his name tag: David Bernz. Officer Bernz lived with his twin sons, Jesse and Jacob, about three blocks from Frances' house. He probably knew about the rocks and the garage.

"Are you going to let me in?" he asked through the screen.

Silently Frances got up and opened the door. The officer nodded at her, then waited for Blue to get off the phone.

Frances wanted to be arrested. If anything happened to Everett, she wanted to be thrown into jail forever. No punishment would be bad enough if she had caused him harm.

"Idaho or Wyoming," Blue said when she hung up. "For fifty dollars that's about as far as he could get. Hey, Dave." She handed the officer a picture of Everett. It was his latest school picture. He wasn't smiling; Everett didn't believe in smiling for the camera.

"Cute," the officer said. He turned to Frances.

"He's only eight." Frances was waiting for him to dust for fingerprints or send some bloodhounds out on the scent of Everett's clothes. Wasn't he supposed to be doing something? Anything but standing quietly in Blue's kitchen looking at a picture? "I know it's my fault he ran away," she said. "I sent him money, and he said he would never disappoint me. He said I could count on him."

Officer Bernz pocketed the picture. "Can you think of anywhere he would go, other than back toward his mother or here? Are there other relatives or friends between Oregon and Ohio? People he trusts?"

Blue and Agnes and the officer all turned toward Frances.

"No," she said. "Everett trusts everyone. But we don't have any other family. There isn't anywhere else in the country he'd want to go."

Agnes stayed for dinner that night, although they never ate dinner. Mrs. McGuire drove over with a pot of stew, dished it into bowls, and set it on the table. No one touched it. Blue thanked her and eventually put the entire pot into the freezer. Even George, Agnes' cousin, offered to help, calling to ask whether he could look through Everett's room for additional photos or an address book or other clues.

Sixteen hours had gone by, and no one had seen him. Frances tried not to picture him lost in the woods or wandering around in a city by himself. She wondered if he had lost his glasses. He didn't see very well without them. Sometimes he even forgot he was wearing them, and fell asleep with them on.

Frances spent most of the evening sitting in the semidark at the kitchen table, while Blue read the same page of the newspaper over and over, and Agnes quietly shuffled a deck of cards. Whenever the phone rang, all three of them jumped. But it wasn't Everett. Twice in a row, it was Frances' mother. Frances didn't want to talk to her, but the second time she called, Blue put an arm around Frances' shoulder and held the phone to her ear.

"Frances." Her mother's voice was quiet, but steady. "I don't want you to panic. We've searched every building, but we're going to keep looking. We're going to find him. I'd come back to stay with you, but the police say I need to wait here in case he comes back to Mountain Ash."

Frances sat still but didn't answer.

"You know how determined he is," her mother said. "I think he gets that from you."

"You weren't watching him," said Frances. She took the phone out of Blue's hands and held it herself.

"I checked on him," her mother said. "He'd left his light on, and I went into his room and turned it off."

"You didn't check on him in the morning." Frances was gripping the phone so hard her knuckles hurt. "I guess you forgot."

"No, I didn't!" her mother said. "I looked in, and I saw the covers all bundled up, and I thought he was asleep. Frances, I don't want you to think we aren't going to find him."

"*You* aren't going to find him," Frances said. "For twelve hours you didn't even notice he was missing."

Blue stood up and came toward her, but Frances dodged her and carried the phone into the dining room. She had been trying to stay calm, but now felt a boiling rage rise up the length of her body. "You couldn't tell the difference between Everett and a lump in the covers. Blue already told you to watch him . . . I warned her he was going to run away. And he ran away from *you*. He didn't want to be out there. He ran away because you lied to us about how long you were going to stay. You took him away from the place where he was happy, and you split us all up and took away the things I sent him for his birthday, and *he hated that*! He hated Oregon! But you pretended he didn't. You lied to us about coming home. How could you have any idea where to find him if you couldn't even—"

Blue grabbed her arm and finally wrestled the receiver away. "We shouldn't tie up the line anymore, Anna-Louise," she said, holding the phone out of Frances' reach. "Yes, she's all right. She's fine. All right, I will." She carried the phone into the kitchen. "I'll tell her. Good night."

Frances sat down again, across from Agnes, whose eyes were as round as boiled eggs. She felt her entire body shaking.

"Your mother wants me to tell you that she loves you," Blue said. Then she hung up the phone.

At nine-thirty Mrs. McGuire came to pick up Agnes. She brought more food: a pan of brownies, a thermos of coffee, and a quart of chocolate milk. She washed all the dishes and wiped the counters and swept the floor, and when Blue stood up to look for a dish towel, Mrs. McGuire hugged her.

Frances watched them, Blue awkward and stiff with her big hands patting Mrs. McGuire's shoulders. They almost looked as if they were dancing.

Then Agnes hugged Frances. "Call me," she said. "I'll be back tomorrow."

Frances nodded. She listened to their car as it pulled away. For a few minutes she looked at the phone, willing it to ring. When it didn't, she walked down the hall to Blue's study. Blue was arranging a pile of blankets and pillows on the extra mattress on the floor. "I thought we could sleep in here," she said. "You take the bed. That way both of us will be able to hear the phone."

Frances looked around the room. She didn't care where she slept. She didn't want to sleep. Sleep seemed like something she had outgrown. "Do you think we'll find him?" she asked.

Blue sat down on the pile of blankets. "This is Everett we're talking about. *He's* going to find *us*."

They left the kitchen light burning. It cast a soft gold net into the dining room and over Blue's feet, which nearly extended through the door.

chapter fourteen

Though Frances wasn't sure whether she slept that night, her mind conjured up a number of different dreams. In one, she was walking through a bus station full of people, all of them holding Everett's picture and calling his name. In another, she and Everett were about to go sledding with their father, the three of them poised at the top of an endless hill, everything around them empty and white. "Jump off and push us," her father said, so Frances did. She jumped off the sled and put her hands on her father's back. The sled started moving, her father and Everett gliding away from her down the slope. She ran after them and shouted, but she couldn't catch up. She heard them laughing together in the distance, their voices like bells.

Like ringing. Like a telephone. She struggled up in the darkness just as Blue flung off the blankets and leapt up from the floor. The two of them collided, Blue's elbow catching Frances in the ear.

"Hello?"

Frances disentangled herself from the blankets. Her ear was throbbing. "Who is it? Have they found him?"

"Hello?" Blue was holding the receiver. "No one's there."

Frances looked at the clock. It was four A.M. Everett was somewhere in the middle of the country on his own.

"I think it only rang once," Blue said.

Frances stared at the phone. Why hadn't they slept with their hands on the receiver? Why had they gone to sleep at all? "It might have been twice," she said.

Blue shook her head. "No. Once. And it could have been a wrong number."

Frances didn't say anything, but she knew it had been Everett. For some reason he had called, then quickly hung up. She and Blue stood in bare feet and T-shirts, squinting in the light Blue had switched on in the hall.

"Do you want to go back to bed?" Blue asked.

"No." Frances shook her head.

"I don't either. And I don't think I could get any work done. How about you?"

"I don't have any work to do. I'm eleven."

"True. Are you hungry?"

Frances didn't want to be hungry, but her stomach reminded her that she hadn't eaten dinner the night before. "A little."

Blue took Mrs. McGuire's stew out of the freezer and tapped it against the counter. It was solid as a rock. "How about brownies?" She took two forks out of a drawer and lifted the tinfoil from the metal pan. "I don't think we need to cut them. It's just us." She drew a line across the middle of the pan with a fork. "This is my half. That half's yours."

They began eating from the edges toward the center. Frances' mouth got tired along the way.

"Do you remember when Everett was little, and he used to hold on to your hair instead of a blanket?" Blue asked. "I always wondered why that didn't bother you."

Frances remembered the feeling of having Everett behind her, a little shadow. She remembered the gentle tugging on her hair.

Blue poured two cups of lukewarm chocolate milk from the carton they had left out all night. "We can call Anna-Louise in a couple of hours," she said.

Frances didn't answer.

Blue leaned back in her chair and put the milk into the refrigerator without standing up. "We'll see if she's heard anything. She'll have talked to the police out there by six or seven."

"She's probably too busy working in the kitchen to worry about Everett," Frances said.

Blue's chair clacked down on the wooden floor. "I know you don't believe that."

"Anyway, it's lucky that Everett was the one to run away, instead of me." Frances reached up over the kitchen table and pulled on the string attached to the light. "If I ran away she probably wouldn't notice."

Blue leaned forward so that her face was uncomfortably close to Frances'. "Your mother would sacrifice her life for you in a second."

Frances turned the light off, then on again. "What's that supposed to mean?"

"It means she's doing the best she can. It means no one is perfect." Blue sipped her milk and some of it dribbled onto the table. "It means that if the two of you have trouble getting along sometimes, it's probably because you're so much alike."

"We aren't alike," Frances said. "We're completely different. I'm a slob and she's neat."

"She was a slob when she was your age," Blue said. "And both of you are stubborn. Both of you are determined. You both love Everett."

Frances put down her fork and pushed the pan of brownies away. "I feel sick," she said. She noticed a row of paint cans—shiny new ones—lined up by the door. "Where did those come from?"

"I bought them," Blue said. "I'm going to fix up the other half of the attic. The big closet."

"What for?"

"An extra bedroom. In case you and Everett ever want to spend a weekend here with me. That way you can each have a room of your own."

Without knowing she was going to do it, Frances started to cry. She was sobbing, her head on her arms on the kitchen table.

"Hey," Blue said. "If it's such a terrible idea, forget it. I take it back."

"No, don't," Frances said. She sat up and sniffed, then wiped her face on her sleeve. "What color are you going to paint it?"

Blue shrugged and looked at the row of cans. "I figure

we can let Everett make that decision. You can be the one to ask him when he gets home."

The phone rang all morning. Frances' mother called twice. Blue talked to her both times and told Frances that she didn't have any news. Then Agnes called, asking whether anything had happened. "I'll be over at ten," she said. "My mother's driving me over with some more food."

Frances had just started to help Blue clean the attic closet—they had to keep themselves busy, Blue said—when Officer Bernz called to ask Frances a number of questions she had already answered. Had Everett told her where he was going, exactly? Was Frances sure about his handwriting on the card? How much money did he have with him?

Then someone called and hung up. Frances let out a shout that brought Blue running down from the attic closet with a mess of cobwebs in her hair. Both of them stared at the receiver.

"We need a new phone," Blue said. "I'm going to call the phone company and then go out and buy one. In an emergency, they should be able to hook us right up. Caller ID," she explained, reaching for her car keys.

But Frances took them away from her, and convinced her to let Mrs. McGuire buy the phone instead.

By late afternoon, there were three working phones in Blue's tiny house, one of them a new cordless with a little gray window in the receiver. Blue had cleared out the attic. The closet was just big enough for a bed and a dresser. Frances and Agnes swept it out, then sat on the porch and played at least twenty games of Chinese checkers. Frances felt as if her head was full of plastic multicolored pieces rattling around.

Cars had been pulling up into the driveway between the graveyard and the house. People came to the door offering to hang up pictures of Everett, to make phone calls or run errands or bring food.

Blue said she hadn't talked to so many people in a single day since she'd been in high school. For the first time all summer, the bank of computers on her desk sat dark and unused.

"School starts in three weeks," Agnes said, after Everett's old teacher, Mrs. Bettsworth, came to drop off some clay figures Everett had made in class the year before.

"I can't even imagine going to school," Frances said. It seemed like years since she had been there.

"Your move," Agnes said. She had set up another game of Chinese checkers.

Frances moved a yellow marble, and Agnes moved an orange one. Frances remembered the last time she had played with Everett—really played, rather than baby-sat or argued with. They had built a motor from a set of batteries and a length of copper wire, Everett methodically connecting one part to another, not really needing her help as she read the directions out loud. Soon they had hit upon the idea of making a robot, and Everett was digging through his LEGOs while Frances ransacked the basement for extra batteries and copper wire. In the end, the robot hadn't worked, but they had spent several hours on the effort, Frances jokingly referring to Everett as Dr. Frankenstein.

Now she thought that although Everett hadn't managed to breathe life into a robot, he had breathed it into Frances and their mother. In their little threesome, Everett was the engine, the spark. She tried not to imagine their family without him.

"Nope, bad move," Agnes said. "You should try to trap me over here."

Frances looked down at the Chinese checkers. She couldn't remember which marbles were hers, or where they were headed, or why a person would want to arrange a bunch of circular pieces on a metal board. "You're losing on purpose, Agnes. It doesn't make me feel better if I win."

"Maybe not. But it makes me feel a little better if I lose."

"All right." This seemed reasonable. "You can lose."

"Thanks," Agnes said. She moved one of her orange marbles directly into Frances' path. "You know, it's only been one day. Everett's probably on a bus somewhere, and all the bus stations are looking for him. He probably hasn't even had time to get hungry yet."

The thought of Everett being hungry at all made Frances want to refuse to eat until he was found. She thought guiltily of the brownies she had eaten in the middle of the night.

"I'm sending an e-mail to Anna-Louise," Blue called from inside the house. "Do you want to add anything?" Now that Everett was missing, Frances' mother apparently was allowed to use the Mountain Ash computer whenever she liked. She was sending messages every hour, some of them to Blue, and some to Frances. Blue printed these out and handed them over, but Frances folded them in half without reading a word.

"No. Nothing," Frances said.

"Tell her to keep her chin up," Agnes called.

Blue's head appeared at the window.

"That's what my dad says. 'Chin up.' It's a saying," Agnes said.

"I'll tell her that Agnes McGuire sends her best wishes." Blue started typing.

The phone rang. It was someone selling lightbulbs that were supposed to last for a dozen years. Ten minutes later Blue took a prank call—a boy who said he was Everett, then laughed and hung up—and she got so angry her hands were shaking when she put down the phone.

"I need to go cut up some firewood," she said. She set one of the phones on the porch floor right next to Frances.

"You don't have a fireplace," Frances told her.

"I think she's going to build one," Agnes said.

Blue tied her bootlaces into double knots and picked up an axe. Soon the sound of chopping echoed against the graveyard wall.

Agnes put away the Chinese checkers and set up a

round of double solitaire. She began playing both sides, turning Frances' cards when Frances forgot. She was already arranging things so that she would have to lose again. "Do you think—" she began.

But then the phone rang. Or rather, Frances felt that it was going to ring. She felt it vibrate on the floor against her foot. Before either she or Agnes heard anything, she had snatched up the receiver. Without thinking, she whispered, "Everett?"

No answer. But there was someone on the line. She could hear him breathing.

Agnes sat watching her, frozen, the playing cards slowly falling from her hands.

"If this is someone pretending to be my brother, I will find out who you are and I will track you down. If this is your sick idea of a joke—"

"It isn't a joke," a voice said. "It's me. Everett."

Frances was clutching the phone with both hands. "Tell me when your birthday is. Tell me our mother's middle name."

"Mom doesn't have a middle name. It's just Anna-Louise. Is that you, Frances? You sound different. Your voice is lower."

"Oh my god, Everett, where are you?"

Agnes seemed to have grown wings. She shot up off the floor. Without touching the steps she vaulted off the porch and disappeared around the corner of the house.

Frances plugged one ear to drown out her screaming.

"I'm still in Oregon." Everett sounded far away and

tired. "I thought I could get a ride in a truck. But I couldn't tell which way they were going. Trucking out here is very unorganized."

"Everett, the police are looking for you. Are you all right?"

"I called you a couple of times," he said. "But I hung up because I didn't want anyone to hear me talking." There was a silence. "I don't really like it out here. It rains too much. And this summer we've had a larger than average rainfall."

"Tell me where you are," Frances said. "I have a plane ticket. I can come get you."

Frances heard Blue pick up the extension.

"I knew the telescope wouldn't work," Everett said. "I just pretended to believe you. I just liked the idea."

"Everett," Frances said. "Were you coming home? Were you coming back here to see me?"

"I wanted to surprise you, Frannie," he said. "You aren't surprised."

"I am, though. Really." She heard the sound of trucks or large engines on Everett's side of the line. "I'm very surprised. I'm amazed, Everett. But you have to tell me where you are."

"I was going to call you up from our house." Everett's voice was quiet. "And I was going to invite you over."

"That would have been fun."

"I might still do it," Everett said. "Mom can come, too. I wanted it to be all three of us. I was going to wait until I got there to call her, but I don't want her to worry."

“All right, then,” Frances said. “So we’ll come and get you.”

A recorded voice came onto the line and asked the caller to deposit a dollar and thirty cents.

“I think I’m running out of quarters,” Everett said. “Tell mom I called.” Then he hung up the phone.

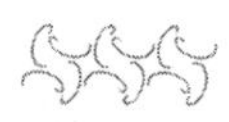

Frances clutched the receiver. “He didn’t tell me. I can’t believe it. The phone went dead. He could be anywhere.”

“No, he couldn’t.” Blue came out of the study with a piece of paper in her hand. “I got the number. The area code is Portland.” She took the phone away from Frances and began to dial.

“Who are you calling?”

“The number he called from, the police, and Anna-Louise, in that order.” Blue was smiling. Her shirt and her hair were flecked with wood. “He wouldn’t have called us if he wasn’t ready,” she said. “This is when we find him and bring him home.”

chapter fifteen

“A truck stop,” Frances told Agnes. “I can’t believe it. He was hiding at a truck stop in a pile of tires. I should have thought of that. Everett loves trucks.”

Blue was humming in front of the computer, e-mailing people to let them know that Everett had been found. He had walked about four miles away from Mountain Ash to Ernie’s Trucks, then spent the day hiding among the tires. The police had found him asleep and filthy at the bottom of a stack of black rubber rings. They’d had to lift the tires up one by one to reach him. When they lifted the last one off, the officers said, Everett’s eyes were still closed, and he was clutching a carton of apple juice and a cherry pie.

“A stowaway,” Agnes said. “Like on a ship.”

“But he wasn’t going anywhere,” Frances said.

“He was trying to,” said Agnes. Everett had told the officers that he’d been waiting for a truck that was open in the back, so he could climb into it. But he’d fallen asleep while he was waiting.

Blue dropped an e-mail message into Frances’ lap. It

read, *Packed. Leaving in two hours. Love to Frances. I wish she would talk to me.*

"What does she want to talk about?" Frances asked.

Blue walked away and didn't answer. A few minutes later she came back with another e-mail. Under the heading, *Frances is asking what you want to talk about*, was a reply.

We can talk about plans for the fall. About staying in Whitman. Tell her I would never have stayed in Oregon without her. Not in a million years.

"This is from my mother?" Frances asked.

Blue nodded. "I can keep walking back and forth like a messenger boy, or you can put your own rear end into that chair and type for yourself."

Frances took a deep breath. She pictured her mother at a computer more than a thousand miles away, her hands on the keyboard, waiting. Maybe Everett was right beside her, watching the screen. Frances stood up and walked to the study, then plopped herself in the chair in front of the monitor. She began to type. She started a number of different sentences, but deleted them. She ended up writing, *Summer was terrible here. Lots of things went wrong. But Aunt Blue was nice to me—none of the bad things that happened were her fault.*

She hit the Send button and waited. Two minutes later a little envelope lit up in the corner of the screen. She clicked on it. *Summer was wonderful here in some ways*, her mother wrote. *The only thing that spoiled it was that you weren't with us.*

Frances studied that final sentence for a while. She could hear Agnes and Blue in the kitchen, laughing and talking. She missed her mother. Her hands began to type before she had time to think about what she was writing. *Agnes asked me why we didn't have Daddy buried in the graveyard*, she wrote. *I told her I'd find out*. She had to wait a little longer for the next reply.

You can tell Agnes that we had a service. Almost everyone in town showed up. There was a lot of music, all of his favorite songs. I think that's what he would have wanted: music and the people he loved, together. Everett sat on my lap, and you sat with Aunt Blue.

Frances wished she could remember it. She wished she could remember the music that her father had loved. She put her fingers back on the keyboard. *I think you and Aunt Blue should learn to get along*, she typed. *It would set a good example for me and Everett*. She pushed the Send button.

A moment later she got an answer. *Of course you're right, Frances. I'll try.*

Frances smiled. Her mother hadn't even bothered to correct her grammar. Instead of "me and Everett," both of them knew she should have written "Everett and me."

About two hours after they had started driving, Everett called from a pay phone at a gas station. "We need windshield washer fluid," he said. "And we're buying sandwiches. This time we have a lot of quarters for the phone."

"Don't get carsick," Frances told him. "Look outside. Keep your window open."

"I won't get carsick," Everett said. "I know where I'm going."

Frances thought that knowing where you were going had no relation to being carsick, but she kept her opinion to herself. She told Everett she was glad he was coming back, even if he had made some friends in Oregon.

"They weren't friends. They were just people my age," Everett said.

"Did anyone out there—you know—do anything strange to you?" Frances asked.

"Like what?"

"Like give you drugs, or hypnotize you, or things like that."

"They gave me aspirin once," Everett said, "when I had an earache. Mom's paying for the gas now."

"So they weren't mean to you?"

"The gas is sixteen ninety-five," Everett said. "She'll get a nickel back from seventeen dollars."

"Everett!"

"No, they weren't mean. They took a lot of walks. They aren't bad people."

"They took away your creatures," Frances reminded him.

"That's because I wouldn't share them. I stole them back from someone who borrowed them, and then he hit me. Mom told me I had to mail them home. Do you want to talk to her?"

It was amazing, Frances thought. She had worried about Everett for most of the summer. And while he was hiking and swimming and playing, she was breaking windows. Throwing rocks. Making a mess of everything. "Then why did you leave?" she asked. "If it wasn't terrible, why did you run away?"

"Because he missed you." It was Frances' mother. "He wanted to see you. Six or seven weeks doesn't sound like a very long time, but when you measure it out in mornings and afternoons, it's a different story."

Frances scratched at some splotches of paint on her fingernails. "Do you wish you hadn't gone?" she asked. She was almost afraid to wait for the answer.

More than a thousand miles away, she heard her mother breathing. "If I hadn't gone, we wouldn't be having this conversation," she said. There was a pause. "Some mistakes are worth making."

"How do you tell which mistakes those are?" Frances asked. But she had spoken too softly, and her mother didn't hear.

"Perfect!" Agnes clapped her hands. "Everything's perfect. They'll be back in two days, and your brother's fine. It's a happy ending. You're staying in Whitman forever and ever."

"I don't know about forever and ever," Frances mumbled.

Agnes ignored her. "We'll be in junior high together. I

don't know what I would have done if you'd left. I would have had to dress up a scarecrow in your clothes and put it on the porch to have someone to talk to."

"A scarecrow," Frances said. "Thanks a lot."

"Well, a doll or something. But now you're definitely staying. I'm so relieved. Aren't you?"

"Sure," Frances said. But she had expected to feel more relieved. Her mother hadn't sounded very definite on the phone. What if the following summer she found another important mistake that just had to be made? Thinking about it made Frances' head hurt. She had always felt that parents should be unchangeable and steady. They should be like fixed points in the sky, the kind sailors used to rely on. But maybe they weren't. Maybe if you looked at them through Everett's telescope, they would be full of pits and flaws, liable to tumble out of the sky without any warning.

"You're happy, aren't you?" Agnes asked.

Frances nodded. She was glad that her mother was coming home. But the fact remained that she had left. And Frances would always feel her leaving like a scar.

The day before Everett and her mother were due back in town, Frances and Blue drove over to the house to clean it. They had to move a cardboard sign to get in: WELCOME BACK, CRESSENS! In the wobbly black Magic Marker lettering, Frances recognized Agnes' hand.

As it turned out there wasn't much to clean, because George had left everything thoroughly swept and scoured.

Frances regretted thinking about him as an overgrown rabbit. He had even left them a vase of flowers in the hall.

As she checked the bedrooms and the shower and the tub, Frances wondered why the rooms seemed empty and sterile. Why was every wall in their house painted light gray or white? And why hadn't she ever noticed it before? Though she didn't touch her mother's things (her mother would want to unpack everything herself), Frances set Everett's collection of rubber creatures very carefully along his shelf.

"He'll appreciate that," Blue said.

Frances looked at Glue-Boy, at Moon-Face, at Banana-Girl. "Where did you get the nickname Blue?" she asked.

"High school." Clumsily, Blue dusted the radiator next to Everett's bed. Frances had never seen her dust. "It was better than Mopey. That's what they called me at first. I guess I looked sad or depressed."

"Were you?"

"Probably." She tucked the dust rag into her pocket.

"You aren't depressed now. You should change your name back," Frances said. "You shouldn't let people call you Blue."

"I don't mind it." Blue shrugged. "And I don't particularly think of myself as Barbara Lee anymore."

Frances finished setting up the creatures, and together they headed to the kitchen, which was very clean. Still, Blue wiped a rag over the counters. Then she opened the door that led to the garage. "Do you think there's anything we need to do out there?"

Frances looked at the stacks of boxes, labeled with her mother's perfect printing. *Winter blankets. Extra hangers. Shoes.* "Probably not." She was about to turn away when she saw a small black box with some kind of silver ribbon around it. Someone had carefully set it on top of the others. There was no label on it, no writing.

Blue was standing close beside her.

Frances looked at the box. It was the right size, the right shape. "I think we should leave all those things for my mother," she said. They shut the door.

Her mother had left a message on the answering machine while they were out. So far they had made good time, she said. She wasn't tired, and the roads were fine, so they were going to stop for dinner and a nap in the car, and then continue on until morning.

"Isn't that a bad idea?" Frances asked after Blue played the message.

"I don't know. Why?"

"Because she'll fall asleep. People who drive all night fall asleep at the wheel."

"Do you want to try to call her back? She left the name of the restaurant. They might still be there."

"No. You call her."

"I'm not the one who's worried about her," Blue said.

Frances went to bed late that night but couldn't sleep. She lay on her back in the attic room, looking out the eight-sided window at the sky. The dials of the clock on the nightstand were glowing green: It was three A.M. She wondered if she had lost the ability to keep normal hours, to eat and sleep on a regular schedule, something her mother felt very strongly about. A few minutes later she heard footsteps on the stairs.

"You're up," Blue said. "Good. I thought I was going to have to wake you."

"What's the matter?"

"Nothing. I just thought we might have a snack. Do you have your shoes on?"

"I need my shoes for a snack?"

"I'll wait downstairs," Blue said. "Just put them on."

Frances laced up her sneakers and pulled a sweatshirt over her pajamas. She found Blue waiting for her by the door. "We aren't going fishing again, are we? That isn't our snack?"

"No. Fish aren't reliable, I've discovered." Blue held the door open and they stepped out into the night. It was perfectly quiet. No crickets, no wind, no trucks going by on the road.

Blue was carrying a pack on her shoulders. Frances followed her along the graveyard wall and in through the open metal gate. They stopped under a clutch of trees and Blue took off the backpack, setting it carefully on the ground.

"What are we doing here?" Frances asked.

Blue took a cloth out of the backpack, shook it, and spread it out in an empty space between two groups of stones. Then she took off her shoes and used them to hold down two corners of the cloth. In the dark, for a big person, she suddenly struck Frances as very graceful. Maybe she was only graceful out-of-doors.

Blue had opened the rest of the pack and was taking out bundles and bags. She produced several plates, napkins, and pieces of silverware, and a huge amount of food: cucumbers with salt, deviled eggs, tuna sandwiches, chocolate cupcakes, radishes, and celery sticks filled with cream cheese and peanut butter.

"You cooked," Frances said. "You made all this."

"I bought the cupcakes. But everything else is homemade. I thought we should have a last feast together, just us two."

"It doesn't have to be the last one," Frances said. She was surprised to find that she was hungry. She started with the eggs, then moved on to the sandwiches and the cupcakes, washing down the food with lemonade. A quarter moon hung above them like a pendant.

"Aunt Blue," Frances said. "Thanks for having me this summer."

Blue's face was barely visible in the darkness. "I wouldn't have missed it."

"I'm glad she's coming back," Frances said. "But I wish most of this hadn't happened. I wish everything could go back to the way it was."

"That's one of the amusing things about life," Blue said. "There's no Rewind button." She put the cups into the backpack. "We have to figure things out as we go."

Frances remembered Mrs. Voorhees, the librarian,

telling her that the purpose of religion was to make sense of your surroundings, to believe in something, to give life a shape. Frances' father had believed in music. Everett believed in nature. Blue probably believed in the view from her study window, the sight of the sun rising over the graveyard wall.

Frances thought that what she believed in most was the idea of her mother and Everett and herself at the kitchen table together on Albion Street. Not that every day was perfect, not that they didn't annoy each other or disagree. But she believed in the fact that they were together, that a rhythm existed in their lives, like a metronome behind a curtain. She craved that quiet rhythm now: the waking up together, the smell of her mother's strong coffee, the sound of the radio at the edge of the kitchen counter, and Everett humming as he lined his fantastical rubber creatures against the wall.

Frances found a soft patch of grass and combed her fingers through it. Maybe the things she loved most weren't meant to be permanent. Maybe the fact that they existed was enough. She lay down on her back.

"What are you doing?" Blue asked.

Frances was flapping her arms and legs. She moved stiffly at first, and then more gracefully, as if she were flying. "Agnes and I learned how to do this," she said. "It's a grass angel." Blue stood and watched her. "It won't last very long," Frances said. "But you can mark the spot in your memory."

Blue waited patiently until she was finished, then

pulled her to her feet. Together they climbed onto the graveyard wall. They were just high enough to see headlights moving along the main road in the distance. "I wonder where all those people are going at this hour," Blue said.

Frances closed her eyes and heard music. She knew who they were, and where they were headed. They were all the people who had been away, and were coming home.

About the Author

Julie Schumacher is the author of numerous short stories and two books for adults, including *The Body Is Water*, an Ernest Hemingway Foundation/PEN Award Finalist for First Fiction and an ALA Notable Book of the Year.

Julie Schumacher is an associate professor of English at the University of Minnesota and lives with her husband and two daughters in St. Paul. This is her first novel for young readers.